P9-DHQ-073

Runners

Runners

David Skipper

VIKING KESTREL

VIKING KESTREL
Viking Penguin Inc., 40 West 23rd Street, New York, New York 10010, U.S.A.
Penguin Books Ltd, 27 Wrights Lane, London W8 5TZ (Publishing & Editorial) and
Harmondsworth, Middlesex, England (Distribution & Warehouse)
Penguin Books Australia Ltd, Ringwood, Victoria, Australia
Penguin Books Canada Limited, 2801 John Street, Markham, Ontario, Canada L3R 1B4
Penguin Books (N.Z.) Ltd, 182–190 Wairau Road, Auckland 10, New Zealand

First published in Great Britain by Walker Books Limited, 1987
First American Edition
Published in 1988

Printed in the United States of America by Arcata Graphics, Fairfield, Pennsylvania
Set in Bembo
1 2 3 4 5 92 91 90 89 88

Library of Congress Cataloging-in-Publication Data
Skipper, David. Runners.
Summary: Fifteen-year-old Jim Taylor becomes the
target of revenge when he finds a computer disk
containing vital drug trafficking information stashed
in a record sleeve borrowed from the library.
[1. Mystery and detective stories] I. Title.
PZ7.S62816Ru 1988 [Fic] 87-21028
ISBN 0-670-81994-8

Runners

I could never have predicted what was about to happen.

Monday morning started pretty much the same. Up at nine. Dressed and ate and out canvassing by half past.

The weather wasn't too bad—not hot, but one of those late days in summer which seem all the better because you know it might be the last decent one before winter sets in.

By ten o'clock I'd gotten rid of over half my leaflets for the day. I know the owners of a local printing press and they sometimes pay me to deliver their stuff door to door. Today it was for Pritchards, the town's fishmarket.

When I eventually found a phone that hadn't yet been vandalized (and in our housing project that's not as easy as it sounds; there's something about the place that seems to bring out the baser elements in people, a local TV station did a documentary on it once) I called school and told the secretary in my best Irish accent that I couldn't attend because of a broken arm. She was a bit suspicious to begin with because it wasn't the first time I'd gotten bored with lessons and decided to call in sick, but I finally got her to buy it. I don't normally talk with an accent but Irish is one of my better ones. I'm pretty good at voices, probably because my parents were both actors. They never actually taught me how to act but I guess I just inherited the knack. It's sort of in the blood.

When I got home just before eleven, I called out, "Top of the morning to you, Gran," and keeping up the accent asked, "And how the divil are ya?"

The dog stopped its scratching long enough to throw me a startled look but Gran ignored the question completely. She can get really pissed off when I talk like that. She started on at me about how late I got in last night and when I tried to explain she just screamed at me, "Stop talking in that bloody stupid voice. They'll drag you off to the funny farm one of these days, just see if they don't." Perhaps she was right.

I'd lived with Gran for almost a year. Before that I spent some time with Jack and Ellie, an aunt and uncle down south. Looking back, I guess I kind of liked it there, but I don't think I realized how much at the time. Just lately, you know, I've begun to think that maybe that old saying is true: about not really knowing what you have until you lose it. At least that's the way it was for Uncle Jack. Weekdays he was an administrator in one of the busiest hospitals in the area, and weekends he spent his time organizing outdoor pursuits for about sixty typically hyperactive Cub Scouts. Jack stood firm when everything around seemed to crumble into chaos, and I thought he could handle anything—until Aunt Ellie died. It was a heart attack. Real sudden, which I suppose made it worse because no one expected it. I guess there's a point where all of us crack, and when he lost Ellie, Jack reached it. He just fell to pieces and couldn't handle anything any longer. That's how I came to live with Gran. Gran's house was a bit of a dive and she could be a real pain sometimes, but usually it was OK. Even so, I hadn't intended on staying much longer—but it never crossed my mind that I'd have to leave so soon.

To get back on Gran's right side, I agreed that after lunch I'd take her Dostoevsky novel back to the library. I was planning on going there anyway. There's an amateur operetta group in town where I sometimes help out. We were planning to do *West Side Story* next month and I'd decided to get the soundtrack from the record department.

I slipped Gran's book into the pocket of my faded blazer and picked up my Walkman on the way out. I still had a fair number of leaflets to deliver and having some music to listen to makes the job easier. It was Mendelssohn's Italian Symphony today. I've got a lot of cassettes with all sorts of music. I like pop and rock but some classical stuff is OK too. Mendelssohn's nice to work to.

I didn't know it at the time, but while I was canvassing and slowly working my way to the library, Casey was standing in a drafty downtown shop doorway waiting to make a switch with another member of the Collective. I hadn't met Casey yet and knew nothing about the Collective, but Casey told me all about it while we were heading out of town, toward a place called Greenvale.

The Collective was an underground organization that dealt in black-market trade: drugs, pornography, protection rackets. In fact if it was illegal it was a pretty safe bet that somewhere along the line the Collective would be involved.

O'Halloran, the local Collective chief, had assigned Casey to make a switch in the usual spot outside Grey's department store. They often used that spot for switches because it was always bustling with shoppers and if something were to go wrong it was easy to get lost in the crowd.

The switch itself went according to plan. Casey swapped his small, plain-wrapped parcel for an even smaller plain brown envelope about five inches square. He had just moved off and was making his way past the Golden Sun take-out when the cop car screeched to a halt in front of the concrete islands that line the pedestrian precinct. Casey burst into the Golden Sun, jumped the counter and pushed his way through the steamy kitchen and out through the service entrance at the back.

The alley behind the take-out is long and narrow and leads to the border between the smart, commercial areas of town and the more run-down areas of our housing project and the mining land beyond. It is on that border between old town and new that the library stands.

I made it to the library just as Mendelssohn's Italian Symphony was finishing. Taking off my headphones and draping them around my neck, I moved to the entrance; and that was when I saw Casey for the first time.

We passed on the steps. I was going up and here's this kid being led down by two unbelievably tall, uniformed cops, one on either side, and he's looking just about as sick as anybody could. I figured he had been busted for something, but I couldn't decide what. By the look of hopelessness on his face it could have been something which carried a heavy prison sentence, like armed robbery or international terrorism. By the state of his dirty denim jacket and ragged, oil-stained jeans it could well have been vagrancy.

Inside the library I returned Gran's novel and got a real funny look from the girl when she noticed it was Dostoevsky. I guess she was expecting *Chicken Licken Finds a Piece of the Sky,* or something equally intellectual.

I said, in the most upper-crust voice I could, "You simply *must* get more Chekhov in," and glided off to the music section before she had a chance to reply.

Chekhov's another of Gran's favorite authors. She says that he expands the mind, and points out that at her age that's all she wants expanding. I don't know why it was me who had to end up with a Gran like her. It's not that she's batty. She's just never really been content doing the usual things grans are supposed to do, like knitting or baking or listening to the Golden Oldies show on Sunday-morning radio. She seems to go through these weird phases. This time it was classical literature. Before that she'd started watching an afternoon TV show called "Paint Along With Nancy," and that started an oil-painting period which was pretty intense but I'm glad to say it didn't last long, even if it *was* beginning to seem endless at the time.

In the hallway I scanned the community-notice board to see if anything interesting was happening around town; things had become pretty boring lately and I reckoned something was due to happen. Not according to the board. The only new notices were for a children's play schedule and a "bring your own racket" open badminton tournament. I couldn't decide which was the more uninteresting.

Ten minutes after entering the library I left with the original motion-picture soundtrack of *West Side Story* under my arm. Before heading home I stopped at the Golden Sun, totally unaware of the drama it had seen less than an hour earlier. There I ordered a portion of number twenty-seven, which I chose simply because it was the cheapest. It turned out to be egg fu yung and it really wasn't bad, considering that the Golden Sun has a reputation around town for being really bad, but I think that's mainly because it looks more like an inner-city soup kitchen than a small-town Chinese restaurant.

As soon as I got home I went up to my room and started my record player turning. I always have to do that first because, being practically prewar vintage, it takes a while to warm up. It doesn't look like much and isn't even stereo, but it's reliable and serves its purpose OK. And I suppose in my dingy little hole of a bedroom it fits in with the decor pretty well.

While I was waiting for the gizzards of the player to warm up, I decided to give the record a clean. I've collected a lot of records over the years—all different types, from the Ramones to Vivaldi, Minnelli to Mozart—and they're all in excellent condition. Not like the ones from the library which I swear some people must use as Frisbees. Some are so grimy you'd be better off throwing away the cleaning cloth and arming yourself with a good sharp chisel instead.

The square brown envelope dropped to the floor as I slipped the record from its sleeve. I didn't take much notice of it at first because people slip sales leaflets into practically everything these days, and that's just what I assumed it was. Junk mail. Yet something about it kept kind of nagging at me. Maybe it was just what Gran calls "plain nosiness" and I call "natural curiosity." Whichever it was, I've got my fair share of it, and halfway through side one of the soundtrack it got the better of me.

Using my rusty old penknife, I slit the envelope open, and into my lap fell an unmarked, three-inch computer disk.

Later that night it rained.

By the time Casey had left the police station, daylight had faded and the wet streets shone with reflected neon. Casey hadn't traveled more than fifty yards before the car pulled to a halt in front of him. He didn't resist or try to run.

Like he told me later, "You can't resist a .45 Magnum, and you can't outrun a Jag 3.6."

He was taken to the Collective's headquarters, an old, detached building in the center of town, and long before O'Halloran arrived to question him, his lower lip was oozing blood from a gaping split and both his eyes were bruised and swollen.

Next morning I woke earlier than usual and by 8:29 A.M. I was outside the school gates, waiting for the bell to ring and the doors to open. In my left pocket was the envelope that contained the computer disk. In my right pocket was a plaster hand cast I had found in the chest of theater junk that had been left to me by my parents.

The bell rang and the kids shuffled their way inside. I

slipped on the cast. It was a bit big and itched like crazy, but if anyone saw me I'd have my excuse for yesterday backed up. *Yes, sir. Broken in three places.*

If I was lucky and moved along with the crowds, I wouldn't need it.

"Jim?"

McGovern, head of History, passed me on the stairs. I pretended not to hear and continued on up with the rest of the kids. I don't know what it is that makes me stand out from the others. I'm not tall and don't look anything special but people always seem to spot me. McGovern did.

"Taylor!" he called again. Louder this time.

I turned; there was no choice. "Yes, sir?"

"What are you doing on the premises? I thought you were absent this week."

"Yeah, I'm not supposed to be here . . ." I began and held up my arm so the cast could clearly be seen as I racked my brain for an explanation. "But I'm a little behind in math. I figured I could pick up a book and study at home."

It was the best I could think of, and I almost kicked myself for saying it. Surely not even a pinhead like McGovern was dumb enough to buy that one.

He paused a moment and stepped closer. He's one of those people who stand so close when they're talking to you, you could count their eyelashes. I hate that. His breath didn't smell of roses either.

"Very commendable, Taylor," he hissed. "Come and see me when you're finished. I'd like to discuss your history project."

Screw you, McGovern.

"Yes, sir." I smiled politely and headed up the stairs toward the computer room.

When it wasn't being used for classwork, the computer room was out of bounds, primarily because when an independent assessor was brought in to assess the pupils' achievement in computer studies, he had found that they knew precious little about binary numbers although they could beat the hell out of him at Pacman and "Checkered Flag." I knew that the key was kept in the desk of the classroom next door, so that was no problem.

The screen lit up. MY NAME IS LOGAN.

PLEASE ENTER YOUR NAME:

The computer had a password program, so I had to spend almost five minutes entering false names and answering stupid questions that the upperclassmen had programmed into it before I was let into the main system.

I eventually got the all-clear. The problem was that I hadn't attended that many computer lessons and I wasn't really sure how to load the disk into this particular model. First I simply tried to push it into the drive unit, but it went in halfway and wouldn't budge any further. Then I tried several different commands without success and began to wonder if it was worth it. There was probably nothing of interest on the disk. Store invoices maybe, nothing interesting. But if you don't look, you'll never find out. Time was passing, though, and if I didn't find out soon I'd have to give it up as a lost cause.

Eventually, when I couldn't think of anything else, I tried RELOAD, which seemed to do the trick. There was a quiet hum as the disk disappeared into the drive unit and for a moment the screen blacked out. Seconds later it lit with the message: ONE MOMENT. GETTING DIRECTORY.

I did it!

"What are you doing here?"

A whole page of data flashed onto the screen but I switched off the unit before I had a chance to look at it.

I glanced back at the door, the direction in which the voice came. It was a teacher. At least I think it was. I hadn't seen him before. He must have been new at the school.

"Don't you know this area is out of bounds?"

Like an exhausted kangaroo, I was about to say but decided against it. Not the right time.

"I was told to collect the . . . uh . . ." The what? The what? ". . . the attendance disk for Mr. Allen."

At first he looked unconvinced but nodded at the brown envelope in which I had found the disk.

"Is that it?"

I nodded, picked up the empty envelope and was quickly ushered out. Hardly a new experience: sometimes it seems to me that going through school is like one long cattle trek. The teachers are the hardened cowhands. The school is the ranch, and we the pupils are the poor cows in the middle, always being herded from one room to another. Out of one building and into the next. It's kind of hard to see the point sometimes, except I suppose it gives an illusion of progress—even if it is a false one.

When I got back home there was a card slipped into the old wooden frame of the big oval mirror which hung on the living room wall. It read: SHOPPING. DINNER IN OVEN.

I carried the charred remains upstairs to my room to try

and salvage what I could. It might have been a casserole but I wouldn't have put money on it. It's never easy to tell. Gran must rate as one of the world's worst cooks, that's why I eat out a lot.

As I passed Gran's room I was thinking about the disk and what had flashed onto the screen. Had I really seen the word *heroin* before the screen faded or was it just my mind working overtime? I was just about to push my way into my room when something else struck me; if Gran was out shopping, with the dog for company, then who was responsible for the rustling sound coming from her bedroom?

Silently stepping into my room I put the plate onto the bed, slipped off the plaster cast and replaced it in the chest of theater props and after a few seconds of quiet searching, pulled from the chest a blank firing replica of a Colt .45 revolver.

Gran's door squeaked as it opened. The boy who had been searching through Gran's chest of drawers spun around and in the same movement pulled from his back pocket a bright white object which snapped open to reveal the gleaming blade of a polished switchblade.

Even holding the blade, Casey looked more threatened than threatening. His big brown eyes were wide and staring like a startled animal's. His face was badly bruised and his cut lip pouted like one of those cheap paintings of crying children with enormous sad eyes. When I pulled the gun from my pocket he dropped the knife and staggered backward into the chest of drawers he had just been searching.

"Are you crazy?" I asked calmly. He didn't look too

dangerous. "Of all the houses in this street, you decide to break into *this* dive?"

It didn't make any sense; there are about thirty houses on the street, which was initially built as temporary accommodation to rehouse those who lost their homes in the war. Our house is in the middle of the block, and none of the houses on either side are what anyone could call well-situated or stylish, but at least most of the other owners have made some attempts to smarten them up. Inside and out, ours looks much the same as it must have done the year it was built. It's really small too. What real estate agents would call *compact* or *easily manageable,* and what any normal person would call *shabby*. Yeah, old and shabby, that probably sums up the house as well as anything. In other words it just wasn't the sort of place anyone would want to burgle. Gran said it was the best anti-theft device you could get, and she was probably right.

At first Casey stood silent. He just stared at the gun.

Eventually he said, "Your name Taylor?" But he never took his eyes off the Colt.

I nodded curiously. "Why?"

"The disk," he said quickly as if it explained everything, and when I looked a little puzzled he started muttering incoherently about things I didn't really understand. I figured the gun was making him so nervous he had difficulty concentrating on the story, so I placed it back into my pocket and he seemed to relax a little. He told me how he had traced the disk to me through library records and how important it was to get it back. I sank onto the bed and looked at the mess in the room.

"Didn't you ever think of simply asking for it?"

He looked a little embarrassed as he explained that the house was empty when he got here. He didn't have time to waste waiting for someone to show.

"Yeah, well you'll have to wait until after five." I told him and explained about the incident at school. That I was supposed to be sick and couldn't risk going back until everyone else had gone.

If we didn't get the disk back, he announced gravely, we'd both be *real* sick, and it sounded to me like he meant it.

It took some time and more than a little effort but I finally got him to understand that the disk was safely locked away, and that if he met me at the bike sheds at five o'clock we could retrieve it together. No sweat.

Still he looked suspicious. "How do I know you'll show?"

"You don't." I shrugged casually and told him that as I was the one with the gun, he didn't have that much say in the matter.

He quietly left the room the way he had entered. Through the window.

I went back to my room and started *Road to Ruin* turning on my record player. Listening to the Ramones belting out "I Wanna Be Sedated" kind of numbs the senses and usually makes tackling Gran's meals easier. I've got a version on cassette too, so I can eat downstairs wearing my headphones without disturbing Gran. I reckon she'd go wild if she knew the real reason I wear them, I suppose that's why I tell her it's the school's third-year French tape.

I reached the school at about a quarter past five. I hadn't forgotten about our agreement, it just sort of slipped my mind for a while. That sometimes happens when the TV's on or when I pick up a book. When I got to the bike sheds they were empty. I searched the grounds and eventually found Casey prowling around the service entrance at the back of the kitchens. I sneaked up behind him and slapped a hand on his shoulder. I know I shouldn't have but I couldn't resist it. I kind of regretted it afterward because he went really pale, and after the initial shock he seemed like he was really angry and I thought for a moment he was going to sock me one.

"I thought you said five o'clock," he growled at me.

I was glad he didn't have his switchblade. In his rush to get out of the house he'd left it where it had fallen. I intended to give it back to him, but not while he was in this mood.

"I got held up," I lied. It was easier than saying I wanted to see the end of the film. It was the Tuesday matinee, *Lassie Come Home*. It was such a warm, caring story I just got carried away with it. I guess I must be what Gran would call "an old-fashioned softy" at heart. It's just a pity real life can't be like that. Anyway, it may have made me late but it put me in a good mood and anything Casey could say wouldn't bother me.

Casey examined the doors and said they were bolted from the inside. It didn't matter because I knew another way.

"Listen, Taylor," he began as we made our way to the back of the building, "are you sure you know what you're doing? I saw some guy inside earlier. The last thing I need is to be busted for breaking and entering."

I could do without it too.

When we reached the back of the school and were sure

no one was looking, we stopped outside the biology lab. Our school is a big, modern high school, all plate glass and fiberglass paneling. The walls above waist height are plate glass and below that are fiberglass panels. I got Casey to stand watch while I squatted down beside a loose panel on the left, and using his switchblade, managed to insert it between the panel and its metal frame. With a little bit of levering the panel fell out. Not all the panels do that but if you know the right ones it's not difficult to get in. Most kids use it at one time or another, to get into the Thursday evening disco without paying, or to spy on the PTAs. There's a panel on the inside, too, but once you've got the outside one off it's just a matter of kicking around the edges and it'll fall in quite easily.

After we crawled through and replaced the panel, I handed Casey his knife back and told him to take care of it in the future, those things were dangerous. They're illegal too, but it's not too difficult to get ahold of one if you know the right (or wrong) people. A few months ago the school trip to Austria had to be extended by one day when some of the kids were caught trying to smuggle switchblades inside their camera cases.

"And I suppose a .45 revolver isn't?" Casey snapped as he snatched back the knife. He honestly believed that it had been real. I laughed out loud and explained that it was only a stage prop. At first he looked real irritated. Casey could never hide what he was thinking. Everything he felt was reflected in his face as clearly as if it had been written there in bright red ink. At that moment the ink would have said: *Taylor, you bastard. You scared the hell out of me with that thing*. That angry expression didn't last for long.

When he glanced around the bio lab all the hardness drained from his face and it took on a sort of amazed expression, as if he'd never seen anything like it before in his life.

He seemed drawn to the greenish glow coming from the tropical aquarium.

"What is this place?" The same sense of wonder sounded in his voice.

"School."

"Don't look much like any school I've seen."

I glanced around the lab. The scene of so many boring hours. You know even for an actor's kid it's kind of difficult to feign interest in the intestinal workings of the fruit bat for two whole hours. And if it's not bats' intestines it's usually something equally gross. Sometimes I think I should have taken physics instead. I know falling objects and stuff like that can be boring too, but at least it doesn't turn your stomach.

I looked at Casey and shrugged. "Looks pretty ordinary to me. It's the biology lab."

He looked into the locust house. If he had put his face any closer to the glass he would have been in there with them. "It looks more like a zoo," he said as he moved to the gerbil cage.

"You should see some of the pupils," I told him. He was acting really strange. Outside he was edgy and nervous. Listening to every rustle and quiet sound. Wanting to get it over with in double time. But in here you could probably have exploded a howitzer in the room next door and he wouldn't have batted an eyelid.

He laughed as one of the gerbils began gently to nibble his finger. He must have a way with them. Whenever I try that I usually end up with a chunk of flesh missing.

"Don't they have animals in your school?" I asked. I thought all schools had them.

"I don't go," he whispered, slowly and quietly. It sounded to me as if there were a little sadness in his voice.

"Not at all?" I couldn't understand it. He must have been eligible. He didn't look any older than I was, maybe even a little younger.

He shook his head slowly, and began speaking as if he were recalling some distant, half-remembered dream.

"When I was a kid I went to a real school for a while, but that was a long time ago."

There was something in the way he said "a long time ago" that made me think that a lot of things had happened to him since then. Later he told me why: he was born and raised south of the river in a place called Greylands. The prewar slums the town reserved for what some of the people termed its third-rate citizens: the unskilled, the unemployed, and the problem families that the respectable projects couldn't possibly tolerate. You know the sort of place, the no-hope area most working-class towns have but try their best to pretend they don't. A place they hide away like some dark, dreadful secret. Casey's dad took up that good old working-class pastime of heavy drinking when Casey was six, and a year later his mother walked out on them both, leaving them to cope alone. Shortly after that Casey's dad was convicted of some minor offence. What it was, Casey wouldn't say, but whatever it was carried a prison sentence and Casey was taken into Westfield Hall, one of those state institutions for kids from that type of "problem" background. None of the kids there went to the normal schools in the project because they were all considered disruptive and slow. That wasn't true of course. Some were, most weren't, but you know how people like to categorize things. Well, everyone from Westfield was labeled slow so they were never taught anything more taxing than fractions and decimals, and the Dick and Jane books most of us get past in primary school.

Casey turned back to the gerbil cage. "It was never like this."

"Yeah," I said moving to the door. "Well, this place ain't all fish and furry animals."

I carefully opened the door and quickly glanced out to see if the corridor was clear—sometimes the janitor works late, but there was no sign of him tonight. "Come on," I called quietly to Casey, and a moment later he followed me into the corridor.

"There it is." I pointed to the computer room as we came to the top of the stairs. I told Casey it would be locked and got him to wait by the door while I went and searched for the key. By the time I returned, the door was open and Casey was replacing a wallet full of picklocks into the back pocket of his jeans.

He found the computer room less impressive than the biology lab. "Where is it?" he asked, and I noticed that nervous edge creeping back into his voice.

Sitting at the workstation, I tapped the disk drive.

"In here," I said and reached below the desk to switch the power on. Before I had a chance to do anything about it, Casey picked up the drive unit and began tugging hard at the piece of disk that stuck out from it.

"How's it come out?"

And I thought *I* was behind when it came to computer technology.

"Are you nuts? You can't do that." I snatched the unit away before any more damage could be done. Casey looked down at me as if I were the crazy one. I think I must have shouted.

"You can't just wrench it out," I told him more calmly, and was about to explain how delicate some of these systems could be, when something on the monitor distracted me.

STORAGE MALFUNCTION. It flashed green on black and the speaker on the monitor started warbling with a two-tone warning siren.

Casey pointed. "What does that mean?"

I didn't know and wasn't sure how to stop it. The screen went on flashing. I looked from it to Casey, whose mouth was closed but his eyes were saying: *Well, don't just sit there. Do something.*

RELEASE was the only command I could think of. The instant the command was entered, the screen just seemed to drain of all light and the noise from the disk drive changed from its usual quiet purring to a loud persistent grating.

After about a minute, it began to vibrate rapidly.

Casey gave me a puzzled look. "Should it do that?"

I shook my head. "It's a disk drive," I told him, "not a food processor."

"Well, stop it."

The command was so logical, it jarred. Made worse by the fact that I didn't know how to.

"Got any suggestions?" I snapped irritably. I wished I'd attended more lessons.

I started typing whatever commands I could think of onto the keyboard. Some I half-remembered, others I was making up on the spot.

Nothing happened.

The grating noise seemed to be getting louder. I'm not sure if it was real, or just my imagination, but whichever, the sound was beginning to drive me nuts. Apparently, it was having the same effect on Casey because he reached over and pulled the plug. I could have stopped him, I suppose, but it really was getting to me and I was as glad as he was when the grating stopped.

"You shouldn't have done that," I said.

"It stopped it, didn't it?"

"Yeah, but you might have erased the whole disk."

That can sometimes happen when you drain the power suddenly. Casey slumped in the chair beside me and looked like he'd just received a heavy prison sentence.

"It can't be *that* bad," I said, and then, noticing the glazed look in his eyes, added unsurely, "Can it?"

"How bad is bad?" He shrugged. "Couple of broken arms? A shattered kneecap, maybe. That's if we don't end up at the bottom of the river wearing concrete shoes."

I didn't have a clue what he was talking about, but there was something in the way he spoke and said *We* that made my stomach churn.

"What a minute. What do you mean *we?* It's your disk!"

He looked at the carpet. "I told them you had it."

"What?"

"Before I went to your place, I had to call them and tell

them I'd traced it." He shuffled in his chair and looked at me guiltily.

"Told *who?*" My voice rose a note or two.

"It doesn't matter." He sighed and moved to the drive unit. "You sure it won't work?"

I shrugged. "You want me to try it again?"

"No. Just get it out of that . . . that thing and let's have a look."

"You can't tell by looking," I told him. "A full disk looks exactly the same as an empty one."

Casey picked up the drive unit. It seemed like he'd had enough of the entire subject to last him a lifetime. With one strong tug he pulled on the disk and after a brief resistance it released itself.

"Is that what they look like?"

I couldn't tell whether Casey was serious or not but I think even *he* knew that the ragged piece of charred plastic he held in his hand was not an intact computer disk. I pulled a blank disk from a box at the side of the monitor and put it beside the one Casey held. The difference was unmistakable. No warped edges. No misshapen center hole. No carbon coating.

"Jesus!" In one movement, Casey slipped the disk into his back pocket, spun around and made for the door.

"Wait!" I called. "Where are you going?"

"To catch a train." He didn't look back.

"A train?" I had to run to keep up. "Where to?"

"I don't know. Away. South maybe. Anywhere away from here."

He was walking so fast I almost slipped on the stairs trying to keep pace.

We didn't bother leaving the way we'd come in, through the panel. Casey kicked open the first fire exit he came to and I followed him into the playground.

"Can't you just take it back and explain what happened?" I asked, a little breathless.

Casey didn't look back, just let out a bitter, humorless laugh.

Personally, I didn't see what all the hassle was. So one computer disk got ruined. So what? I couldn't understand why it was so important and I told him so. He stopped walking so suddenly I almost ran into him. "That," he snapped, "is because you don't know what it contained or who we're dealing with."

"So who are we dealing with?"

He looked at me a minute without saying anything. It was as if he were deciding whether to tell me, then a car turned onto the road at the front of the school and he took a step back into the shade of the building. His eyes didn't leave the car until it turned off the road at an intersection far in the distance. Then he glanced at his watch and started walking again. "I've got to go. I'll be at the station in an hour. If you're not there I'm going alone."

That churning feeling in my stomach returned.

"I'm not going anywhere," I told him positively. I was through traveling: before Uncle Jack and Aunt Ellie took me in I was staying with Mum's cousin Bob and his wife. They were staying up at the old house near Malton at the time my parents were killed and I suppose to move in with them seemed the obvious solution at the time; I was nine years old and I knew them better than practically anyone apart from Mum and Dad, and I always liked them as friends. Yeah, as friends they were OK. One or two hours, once or twice a week was great, but as substitute parents, well, who could stand in for the parents of any nine-year-old kid? It's kind of hard now to remember much about the beginning—most of my memories from that time are a little hazy, which is really strange because I have a great memory most of the time and can recall vividly things that happened years before and years after, but 1981 is just a misty void to me now. I don't even know if we traveled that first year or stayed up north. You see, Mum's cousin Bob was some sort of contractor with a big national construction company and his job required him to travel a lot. Once one job was finished he'd move us on to wherever the next one was. Halfway across the country if necessary. Sometimes for a month or two. Sometimes almost a year. In the end they figured it was screwing up my schooling too much so I was packed off to Uncle Jack's. Everyone said I needed a more stable environment.

Nobody asked *me*.

"That's up to you," I heard Casey call back. "Just don't tell them where I'm going."

"Them? What are you talking about? Who's *them?*"

The question remained unanswered. Casey leaped the school fence and moved fast into the distance.

I walked slowly home.

When I got there the telephone was ringing. It was Gran saying that the meeting she had gone to at the Community Center was running late and that she wouldn't be back on time. I told her I'd be OK and that I'd fix myself some sandwiches. I'd done it often enough; Gran was always at one meeting or another, today it was the tenants' association. You know, I think a lot of people around our way think she's a little crazy, but I'm sure that's just because she tends to speak her mind more than most and doesn't care who's listening. I reckon if she were twenty years old, she'd be considered a caring young socialist. As it is, at sixty-five they think she's just another batty old lady with nothing better to do than shoot her mouth off.

I hung up and went into the kitchen to fix something to eat.

I doubt if anyone in their right mind would consider sandwiches to be one of their favorite foods, especially when they've been made with soggy white bread that has begun to smell like a stagnant fish tank, and ham so thin you could clearly see your hand through it, but I didn't really mind. It was better than having to endure one of Gran's corned-beef stews, which Tuesday always brought.

I had just made the sandwiches when I noticed the sleek black Jaguar pull up in front of the house. The glass of the car was tinted purple, and it was difficult to see clearly but for some reason I had the strange feeling that the occupants of the car were looking my way. Not in the general direction of the house, but staring straight at me.

I tried to think. Gran didn't receive many visitors and the people we did know could never afford a car like that.

And anyway, if it were someone we knew, they would have gotten out of the car and come to the door.

I looked at the clock. Four minutes had passed and nothing had happened. The car just stood with its engine quietly purring; it was like a spider, waiting to pounce on an unsuspecting fly. I shrugged. I wasn't going to stand around all day waiting to answer the door. I took the sandwiches upstairs and after putting on a record, moved to the window and looked down on the car in the street below.

Both doors opened at the same time and two men stepped onto the street. The older of the two had dark, close-cropped hair and wore an expensive leather jacket. The younger man had longer, straw-colored hair and had on a sheepskin car coat.

There was a loud knock on the front door.

I should answer it, I thought. *It may be important. I should go downstairs and let them in.*

Let THEM in.

I remembered Casey's words.

Just don't tell THEM *where I'm going.*

There was another rap on the door.

I didn't answer it. Instead I moved to the chest of theater props and took out my big encyclopedia. It was a prop used in the play my parents had first worked on together, called *The Bride Screamed Murder.* Outside it looked like a big ordinary encyclopedia, but inside all the pages had been hollowed out, creating a secret compartment. I quickly filled the book with everything close at hand—my cassette player, the fake revolver, matches and wallet.

The front door was kicked open as I was climbing out of Gran's window at the back of the house. The same way Casey had left earlier in the day.

When I reached the railway station, I found Casey sitting on a bench at platform four, the one furthest from the entrance. He was searching through a wallet he had just lifted and hadn't noticed me come up behind him. It took a lot of control to stop myself from giving him a good hard slap on the shoulder to scare the hell out of him. I figured he deserved it after all the trouble he'd caused me—even if it was partly my fault. I don't know why I didn't. Maybe it was because he'd been so nervous earlier.

He jumped when I sat quietly next to him. It was lucky I didn't try and scare him. He might have had a coronary.

"Listen," I told him, "I don't know what kind of trouble you're in, but you've got to talk to those people."

He looked at me as if I'd just asked him to run the four-minute mile.

"It ain't that easy."

"But they're tearing our house apart!" My voice rose sharply yet Casey didn't appear to notice, he just asked if I'd told them anything. I explained that I didn't wait around to discuss the situation.

"Just tell them I had nothing to do with it," I said. I didn't think it was an unreasonable request.

"Nothing to do with it?" This time it was Casey's voice which rose as he looked at me accusingly.

"You were the one who opened their envelope. You took their precious computer disk to school and you were the one who got it stuck in that overpriced cheese-grater."

All that was true enough and I admitted it, but I had to point out that if he hadn't been so heavy-handed and tried to yank the damn thing out, it would probably have been OK.

He didn't seem too impressed with my defense. He shook his head and waved his hand in a dismissive gesture, then let out a long, weary sigh. "It doesn't matter who's to blame anymore. They're not after the disk now. They don't want excuses, they want revenge."

He sighed again and leaned across the bench, burying his face in his arms.

"Oh, God! Why does everything happen to me?"

Even though his voice was muffled through his jacket, I could still hear the gutteral, choked sound it made.

I looked away and turned my attention to the station.

Behind us at platform two, a train was pulling in. Light flashed out from the photo booth at platform three, and at the front of the station . . .

At the front of the station, walking in this direction, were two men. One wearing an expensive leather jacket. The other a sheepskin car coat.

I looked down at Casey. His face was still buried in his arms and he was breathing deeply, the way people do when they're sleeping.

This time I didn't think twice about slapping his shoulder. Nervous or not, there was no choice.

"Casey!"

He sat up so fast it was as if he'd been coiled there, waiting to spring.

"What is it?" His eyes darted all around.

I nodded over to the two men, who had stopped walking and were talking to the guy in the ticket booth about a hundred yards away. Looking out from our sheltered position behind two telephone booths, we could see them clearly.

Casey sank lower into the bench and for the first time I saw him differently. Up until then he had looked younger than he was, sort of baby-faced and innocent. Even with his tough-looking bruises he looked like he couldn't harm a fly. His dark brown eyes were too big and round and trusting. But now those same eyes narrowed warily and his mouth fell into a twisted scowl of hatred. Suddenly, he looked older.

The train behind us began making noises, like it was readying to pull out. Casey and I exchanged a silent glance. We both knew that the only way we could get out of the situation was to make a run for the train and yet we knew that if we ran for it before it started moving, the two hoods might spot us and jump the train themselves. So we waited and watched. The hoods were still busy at platform one, but they were slowly working their way closer.

Casey glanced at the train. "What's keeping it?"

I looked at the big old clock that was suspended from the metal girders above us and couldn't believe that the train had only been in the station a little over four minutes. It felt more like four hours. Like that old saying you sometimes hear: *Time flies when you're having fun.* When you're not, it can really drag.

The men had almost reached the telephone booths when the train eventually started to roll, and they did spot us as we made the run, but by that time the train was moving too fast for them to do anything about it. We'd barely made it ourselves.

I don't know why I felt so relieved to get on that train. I hadn't a clue where we were heading but it was still kind of fun to hang out of the window and give a choice selection of hand signals to those two jerks left on the platform. Just before the train turned the bend I noticed the one in the sheepskin coat kick at a big wire litter basket which fell off the platform and spilled its guts onto the track.

We made our way to one of the empty carriages at the back of the train. If the ticket collector came that far down we could easily hide. Most of the seats in the carriage faced forward but a few at the far end were arranged so that passengers could sit facing away from the direction the train was heading. Where a front-facing seat joined up to a seat pointing backwards, it left a small triangular gap between, about two feet at its point, and long and deep enough to be able to squat into without being seen.

It's one of the tricks you pick up when you spend a lot of time traveling. It usually works and this time there was no reason for the collector to suspect anything.

As the train got underway Casey tried to explain everything that had happened. He was a bit vague in parts and it was clear he didn't like talking about it, but I kept pressing him. After all, those jerks had just smashed their way into my house and forced us both onto a train heading for the middle of nowhere. I figured I had a right to know why.

I finally had to settle for a fairly disjointed version of what had happened. It was still a little vague but I think I got the general picture: Casey was just twelve when he was first approached by one of the lesser members of the Collective. He had just been busted for lifting two packets of Eveready AAs from one of the big chain stores in town and the organization was looking for some kid out to make a little money on the side, without asking too many questions about the risks involved or worrying whether the job was morally right. Off and on, Casey had done odd jobs for the Collective ever since—no longer out of choice. That was obvious from the way he spoke of the system he'd become trapped in. Nobody chooses to work for people they despise. But like he told me, he had no option. Casey knew it, but more importantly, so did they. Usually the job was just delivering stuff, or making a switch if delivering to a specific building was considered too risky. That day he was spotted outside Grey's he had to make a collection. Not the usual thing. That was stressed when O'Halloran briefed him. This was much more important. Casey wasn't told what the computer disk contained, only issued with a good line of threats of what would happen if anything went wrong.

"Something went wrong." He shrugged and shortly after telling me this he stretched out across the double seat and drifted into a restless sleep. He hadn't slept since the night before the switch and as he lay there across the seat of the train he looked like a different person. He seemed more peaceful than I ever imagined he could. All the worry just sort of drained from his face.

That was the difference between Casey and me. I've never been much of a worrier. I've just never seen the point of it. If you've got problems you can either shrug them off and say *to hell with it, who cares?* Or you buckle down and do something about them. Whichever you choose, worrying about it isn't going to help you one little bit.

We had just smuggled ourselves onto a train and we didn't even know the direction we were heading. I sank further into the seat and said aloud, "To hell with it. Who cares?"

It was dark when the train reached the last stop. I still had no idea where we were but I could tell by the condition of the station that it wasn't a major town. It was too small and run-down. It only had one platform.

When I realized the train wasn't going any further, I woke Casey. He sat up and looked around as if he had just come out of a bad dream. "Where are we?" he asked.

The sign said Greenvale, but that didn't tell us much.

"Where the hell is Greenvale?" I asked. I thought Casey might know.

"North somewhere," he said vaguely as we dropped onto the platform. He didn't need to tell me that; there was a cold, northerly chill in the air that I hadn't noticed back home. We must have traveled further than I thought.

Buttoning my jacket, I flipped up the collar and looked around. There was nothing at the front of the station so we slowly made our way around to the back. There was a Beefeater café. It had closed an hour earlier but a warm, savory smell still hung in the air and made my mouth water. I suddenly realized I hadn't eaten any real food since ten o'clock and that was only popcorn which hardly counts. I never got to try the sandwiches I prepared for supper.

"Hey! Look at this."

Casey had found a map. It was embossed on a square of tiles on one wall of the café. It confirmed our suspicions. We were north. Somewhere between the industrial area below and the farmlands above.

"Not exactly the action capital of the world, is it?" I said and tried to make out the area obscured by a layer of black spray paint.

"If you're looking for action, Taylor, just take the next train home."

Casey sometimes had a flair for melodrama that could

put some of my theatrical friends to shame. I looked back at the map. We were only thirty miles from Malton.

"You know it?" Casey asked.

I knew it vaguely. A long time ago.

"I knew someone who lived there once," I said, but I don't think Casey heard. My voice sounded funny and it came out quieter than I'd intended.

"Well, town's that way." Casey looked from the map to the direction of a dark alley of ancient, vandalized buildings across the road in front of us.

I don't know why but railway stations always seem to be located in the sleaziest parts of town.

A car turned onto the road and drove quickly past.

I hadn't realized how dark and quiet it was until it contrasted with the noise and light from the car, made worse by the recent rain that remained in pools on the road, reflecting the white of the headlights and spraying noisily out from the tires.

As the red taillights faded into the distance, we started for the alley. I tucked the encyclopedia tightly under my arm and wondered just what I was getting myself into.

Casey noticed the book. He looked at it suspiciously and asked if I were a grind.

I didn't know what Casey's definition of a grind was, but I doubted whether I fell into that category. It's not that I'm dumb or anything. I can understand the things they teach at school as good as, maybe even better than, most of the other kids. It's just that sometimes it's difficult to concentrate; I'm usually thinking of something else. When the time comes to study, I reckon I'll buckle down and do it.

The alley got darker as it twisted around to the left, but then it led straight onto High Street—which wasn't what you would call a hive of activity but at least it was brighter and more open than the place we'd just come from.

"So what's the plan, chief?" I asked, sounding a lot more cheerful than I actually felt. A hole like this might begin to get you down if you let it. I wasn't going to give up without a fight.

"Over there." Casey nodded to one of the few lit buildings on the street. Why he chose that one, I wasn't sure, there were other places closer.

It turned out to be the only burger joint in town.

"There's one just like it, back home," he told me as we neared it. "I recognized the sign."

I couldn't see how. From the distance we first saw it, it just appeared to be a blur of light. I wondered whether I needed glasses but Casey said he could home in on any burger joint within a mile, and for some reason I believed him.

Inside the burger joint, Casey chose the table furthest from the window, saying we couldn't be too careful. I didn't know who he was expecting to find us in a godforsaken dive like this and I wouldn't have imagined for one minute that, as we sat calmly and studied the menu, a car was following in the direction of the train.

I ordered southern-fried chicken and french fries—which the menu called a Kentucky Special—and coffee. Casey chose two king-size cheeseburgers, with Coke. The waitress did her best to smile, said it would take about five minutes then disappeared behind a beaded curtain. I glanced around. The place was pretty much like the town itself;

cheap, dull, and unfriendly. You know the sort of place. There's one like it in every town. All imitation pine paneling, dirty ashtrays, and cigarette burns in the plastic tabletops.

Apart from Casey and me, and the man behind the counter, there were only three others in the joint and they were together. A man and woman who were probably in their early thirties and their son, who was about eight and a real pain in the neck. His name was Nigel.

"No, Nigel. You can't have the cake *and* the pie. Mummy's already bought you chocolate and Daddy won't be able to take you to the film tomorrow if you wake up with tummy ache."

They were sitting by the window, right at the other end of the room and you could hear everything they said. It was as if they wanted to be heard, like it made them feel important to be noticed.

It went on for about five minutes: Mummy this . . . Daddy that . . . It drove me nuts to think that an anemic little runt like that could demand such attention. I'm glad my parents weren't like that. I'd hate to think what I'd be like now. I scowled and looked at Casey. He was staring in fascination, like he was watching some TV show. I just felt like getting up and saying *Listen, you little bastard, if you don't order the pie, you're going to be wearing it.*

The parents eventually gave in and ordered half a portion of both.

"I hope it chokes him," I announced as our orders arrived. Casey laughed. I think he thought I was joking.

The meal looked better than I thought it would, but that was probably because I hadn't eaten for so long. Right then, one of Gran's mushroom omelettes would have seemed like a feast.

Taking about half his burger in one mouthful, Casey looked warily at my meal and asked through a spray of bread crumbs if I were one of those health-food weirdos. Casey classified anything that needed to be eaten with a knife and fork as health food.

I told him I wasn't. I just didn't like cheeseburgers and Coke. Polishing off the first burger, he reached for the other and found the check under the plate.

"I've just found out why this place is so empty."

"How much?"

"Five thirty-eight."

"So?" It was a little steep for what we got, but we could afford it. The wallet Casey had lifted earlier contained eighty pounds.

"So we're probably going to be stuck here for some time. An extra five thirty-eight could buy us an extra couple of days."

"What do you want to do, make a run for it?"

Casey looked unsure. "What do you think?"

I glanced at the big guy behind the counter near the door.

"I think you should have thought about it before you chose the seats furthest from the exit," I said. There was no way we could have crossed the distance without him suspecting anything, especially with Casey looking so furtive.

Casey could see I was right. He bit another huge chunk from his burger and chewed on it thoughtfully, then his eyes suddenly lit up as if he had just thought of a foolproof solution. After glancing around to see if anyone was within listening range, he moved in close and whispered into my ear, "You still got that gun?"

You've got to be joking, I thought but asked him why. I was curious to know what he was thinking.

"What do you reckon we'd get for armed robbery?"

I couldn't tell if he was serious or not.

"In a dive like this, twenty clams if we're lucky."

I'd decided he wasn't.

He waved his hand. "That's not what I meant."

I knew what he meant, and I was beginning to think he was serious. It was hard to tell with Casey. Sometimes I don't think he knew himself. His eyebrows would join in the middle like he was thinking really hard then he'd suggest something totally outrageous.

"Forget it." I shook my head. If we were going to get out of the door without paying we'd have to think it out. Do it skillfully, not charge out with guns blazing.

"You got a better idea?"

I did have an idea. I wasn't sure if it was a better one, but I figured if we did get into a rumble at least we wouldn't be busted for armed assault.

I asked Casey if he could wheeze.

"Can I *what?*"

"Wheeze. You know. Cough. Sputter. That sort of thing."

Not for the first time he looked at me as if I'd just sprouted antlers or something. I thought it was a fairly straightforward question that deserved a simple yes or no reply, but to save time I decided to explain my idea in detail. I told Casey about a play I'd once worked on with a local theater group called the Wandering Players. Nothing special. Just typical, tacky amateur stuff. To be honest, most of the group couldn't act to save their lives, and the ones that could act a little were always too busy thinking about themselves to bother concentrating on the roles they were playing. I think that's the real difference between amateurs and professionals. My parents were real pros. I don't mean hyped-up, movie-star-type pros, just hard-working theater people who, like most of their kind, never got the recognition they really deserved. Mum gave up the theater when I was born and Dad switched from major stage roles to minor TV parts just to pay the bills. I figured now was the time to follow in his footsteps and do a little acting to settle a bill of my own.

The play I described to Casey was called *Cottonyard Blues*. I told him about a scene from it which called for one of the actors to deliver a really dramatic wheezing fit and then slump unconscious over the table. I asked him if he could do it.

It was like I'd just asked him to stand in the middle of Woolworth's and recite the dirtiest limerick he knew.

"No way!"

It was about then that I began to think it would save us a whole lot of trouble if we just paid the bill like anyone else would have, but it was no use. Casey had made up his mind not to, and once he'd done that it was practically impossible to get him to change it. It wasn't the money. It was a matter of principle. He said if I told him what to say, we could switch roles and he'd try my part.

We spent a couple of minutes deciding how we would do it and by then Casey was keyed-up and as ready as he'd ever be. So the curtain rose.

Picking my plate up from the table, I stood casually as

if I were about to return it to the counter, and when it was at its highest point—about chest height—that's when I let it drop. It shattered on the floor with a terrific crash which was loud enough to get the attention of everyone in the place—even the brat by the window stopped stuffing his face long enough to see what was going on. As soon as the plate hit the floor I began clutching at my collar, gasping and making the same sort of disgusting slurping noises that got John Hurt an Oscar nomination for his role in *The Elephant Man*. I had just caught sight of the horrified expressions of the people by the window when I flaked out over the table and left the rest to Casey. The routine we'd run through was for him to get up and shout frantically at the fat guy behind the counter, "Hey, mister, quick! Call an ambulance, he's a hemophiliac."

Neither of us actually knew what a hemophiliac was but we both agreed it had a good dramatic ring to it, so we decided to use it anyway. As it turned out though, it didn't really matter because Casey got nervous and messed the lines up, shouting, "Mister, mister. He's a hemodactyl. Hurry."

I had to bite my lip to stop from laughing and just hoped nobody could see my shoulders shaking. Getting the giggles is just about the worst thing that can happen to an actor. I guess it stands about midway between forgetting your lines and falling head first into the orchestra pit five feet below. In the trade it's known as *corpsing* and right then I'd contracted as bad a dose as I can ever remember having. Luckily though, the guy had seen me flip and ran for the telephone even before Casey had finished speaking. Seconds later I felt a heavy slap on my back and heard a triumphant yell of "We did it!"

We left the joint with the family of wimps openmouthed and gawking.

Casey was pleased with his performance. Which really wasn't bad. Oh, he screwed up the lines for sure, but even so there had been real concern in his voice, and that was one of the reasons the guy behind the counter had acted so quickly.

Our timing couldn't have been much worse though.

As soon as we hit the street, it began to drizzle. I wondered if it was raining at home and decided to look for a telephone. When I didn't get in, in a couple of hours, Gran would start to worry, and she'd bottle it all up until I got back, then she'd yell like crazy.

The first phone we found was one of those new vandal-proof ones with pushbuttons and no moving parts. Someone had set fire to the main key panel and fused the buttons together. It had taken us five minutes to find the phone and I was pretty annoyed when it didn't work, but then it made me think back to a time not long ago when I had friends who did things like that. They weren't underprivileged or products of broken homes like they try to make out on TV documentaries. They didn't do it because their parents didn't care, or drank or beat them. They were just plain, ordinary kids from plain, ordinary homes who did it because there was nothing else for them to do that would create the kind of excitement and closeness a shared secret like that could give. Vandals never work alone.

The next phone we found—after another five minutes of walking—worked. It rejected the coin a couple of times but I finally got through, although it was a bad line and Gran sounded like she was angry. She said I left the house in a mess and burned a hole in the kettle. I remembered

I'd just filled it when I saw the car pull up. When I climbed out the back, it must've been boiling away.

I said I was sorry and told Gran that I was staying with friends and wouldn't be back for a couple of days. I said I'd bring another teakettle when I got back. She started to say something, then we were cut off. I hadn't realized I was calling long distance. I had more change but didn't call back. I handed a coin to Casey.

"What's this for?"

"We're not going to be back for supper," I reminded him. "Don't you think you should call home and tell them?"

He handed me the coin back, saying quietly, "Who's them?" Then, flicking up his collar, he started down the street.

The rain was more than drizzle now and the northerly wind was blowing stronger. Walking the streets at night is bad enough without heavy rain and cold winds to deal with. We decided to find shelter and wait for the rain to ease.

The doorway of an old department store seemed as good a place as any. It was lit up and when you stepped into the corner, fairly well-enclosed and windproof.

The windows were lit by fluorescent strip lights. The displays to the left were an end-of-season range of garden furniture, barbecues and things. On the right it was mostly electrical stuff. Casey began to point out all the things he'd buy when he won the lottery. Top of his list was a miniature television no bigger than a cigarette box, followed by a waterproof calculator/watch that was displayed in a tank of bubbling water. Then he looked away from the window and asked me how much I thought the gerbil cage we'd seen back at school might cost. I didn't know.

"Ten pounds or so," I guessed.

Ten minutes later the rain got worse and we both sat close against the glass doors with our coats buttoned tight.

Casey was watching some TV show in the reflection of one of the portables in the window display. It was a detective show which I hadn't even heard of, but he seemed to know everything about it. He explained what was going on, who was who, and even gave me the family backgrounds of the two main characters. He knew a lot about that show, what the actors' real names were, what they worked on before and even who wrote and directed it. But he told me it wasn't his favorite. He just knew a lot about TV in general. I guess when you're stuck in a place like Westfield Hall and you're not too hot with a ping-pong paddle there's not much else to do. I know that sounds depressing but I suppose there are worse things than TV that a person can be addicted to.

The detective show finished at 10:30 P.M. and was followed by a local sports feature.

Still the rain thundered down.

I'm not sure what came after the sports show. I think I must have fallen asleep before it ended because all I can remember is waking up with a sharp stabbing ache in my neck.

It was light. There was something green above me and I had no idea where I was. You know how it is when you first wake and you're not sure if you're still dreaming or not. Then my eyes began to focus on the green and my memory drifted back. The green was the tiles on the roof of the doorway and the pain in my neck was from sleeping all night on the cold surface of the stone floor.

I felt a movement beside me, looked at it and another

part of my memory filtered back. Casey was sitting in the same position I'd last seen him the night before, still looking at the reflected TV screen which was now fainter because of the daylight hitting the glass.

I felt awful. All shivery and aching like I was coming down with the flu. I managed to pull myself up from the huddle I'd woken in to a sitting position next to Casey.

"Why didn't you wake me?" I said, but it came out little more than a grunt.

"It's only seven," he told me, not sounding too good himself. Picking up a half-full bottle of milk, he took a drink and passed the rest over to me. As I was noisily gulping it down, some of it bubbled over and spilled down my coat just as a man in a smart business suit passed. He gave me a real funny look, like I was a regular down-and-outer. It was only when I caught sight of my reflection in the window that I realized how bad I looked: my eyes were puffy and still half-closed, my hair was sticking out in all directions and I had spilt milk running down my clothes.

If I'd passed someone like that two days ago, I think I would have stopped and stared myself.

When I asked to borrow a comb, Casey said he never carried one so I had to spit my hair down and smooth it over the best I could. Really it needed cutting.

High Street looked different in the daylight. Somehow bigger and cleaner. More friendly. Reaching up to the old wooden door handle I pulled myself up and felt the pain stab at my neck again. It was so sudden and sharp I winced out loud.

"You OK?" Casey looked up from the TV. He sounded concerned. I guess I must have been louder than I thought. I nodded and immediately regretted it as the pain stabbed again. "Yeah," I groaned. "Have you been up all night?"

Casey shook his head—easily—and I noticed he looked a lot better than I felt. "Just before six," he said. Standing up, he scanned the street and added, "We can't stay here much longer, Jim. We've been getting some weird looks from people passing. Soon as the store opens they'll move us on."

It sounded to me as if he'd had previous experience at this sort of thing. Me, I hadn't been up so early for a long time, let alone out on the streets. I've never been what you could call a morning person. For my birthday Gran bought me a glass drinking mug, on the side it has a picture of Snoopy lying on top of his dog house looking like death warmed over, and the writing beside the picture reads: *I hate people who sing in the morning*. I guess Gran had got to know me pretty well over the twelve months we'd spent together.

Picking up my encyclopedia, which I'd used as a makeshift pillow, I followed Casey onto the street to the only place that was open that early: a small corner newsstand.

To kill time we flipped through a few issues of *Playboy* and *Penthouse* until the ratty-looking guy behind the counter coughed and motioned to a sign taped above the magazine rack. It had a moronic little verse scrawled on it in green felt-tip that said:

IF YOU'RE NOT GOING TO BUY THEM
YOU'RE NOT ALLOWED TO LOOK.

Casey replaced his with the others and I slipped mine into the center pages of a monthly magazine lower down the rack called *Christianity Today*.

Casey bought Coke. I chose a carton of fresh orange

juice and we went dutch on a big bar of chocolate which we decided to save until we found a place where we could sit and eat. Finally we settled on the waiting room of the bus station—not exactly luxury surroundings, but at least the seats that weren't slashed were padded, and after sleeping the night on that hard stone floor, that was as good as a table at the best restaurant in town.

We spent most of the morning in the local library. It was one of the only really modern buildings in the whole town, and its big, mirrored glass front looked all the smarter because it was situated down one of the grimy alleys that ran off High Street.

Inside, I tried to find out what I could about the town from the local books in the reference section, while Casey engrossed himself in a big colorful hardback all about gerbil and mouse rearing.

Apart from the fact that it was prone to flooding and was the birthplace of a minor television celebrity, who was pretty famous in the seventies but now makes a living doing tacky supermarket ads for Australian butter, there wasn't much else to learn about the town and by twelve o'clock we were back on the streets again, looking for Chiltern Avenue.

"What's at Chiltern Avenue anyway?" Casey asked suspiciously. For the first time, he was following me.

"The cheapest hotel in town," I told him. I'd found it in a *Where to Stay in the North* tourist guide. It was under the "No Frills" section.

Turning off one dingy alley we moved along an even worse one. The road there was cobbled and so full of potholes I twisted my ankle twice.

"A hotel?" Casey asked as if he hadn't heard me right.

I nodded. While he had been busy studying the ins and outs of the rodent world, I'd looked at the local newspaper and the weather forecast said rain. I told him another night in a damp shop doorway might finish me off, and it was probably true.

"Well," I said, "it ain't the Ritz, but what do you think?"

We found the hotel and Casey looked over the outside with disgust. To me it looked just like a derelict Victorian slaughterhouse I'd seen in an old film years back. It was as if when we moved off High Street, we stepped back in time about a hundred years. I felt like Nicholas Nickleby. All Casey said was, "I hope it's better on the inside."

It turned out that it wasn't much. The room we'd been given, after forking over the three pounds deposit and signing in, wasn't much bigger than the doorway we had shared, and most of what room there was, was taken by two small, flimsy-looking beds that stood at either end of the room. The only furniture was an old wooden cabinet which was far too big for the place and had one door and both handles missing.

I felt a sharp slap on my back. "You were right, Jim," Casey said as he crashed onto one of the beds, causing the rusty springs to scream in protest. "It ain't the Ritz."

I tried hard to look on the bright side and say something good about the place, but I just couldn't think of anything. I used to think my room at home was a dive, but I tell you, compared with this it was a luxury penthouse. Gran wouldn't nag at me so much if she could see me now.

I began to wonder what kind of people rented rooms like this, and my mind ran riot with visions of mass murderers, Nazi war criminals, and professional hit men. I've always had this active imagination. Sometimes it's so vivid it's scary. A long time ago, when I was younger my parents got so worried they called a doctor, but he just said there was nothing to worry about, and that I'd grow out of it. It hasn't happened yet so I suppose I should be entitled to some kind of refund on the bill.

"I thought all hotels had TVs in them." Casey's grumbling invaded my thoughts. He was staring thoughtfully at a long deep crack that ran the whole length of the ceiling.

"What did you expect in a hotel like this?" I asked, sitting on the bed opposite and resting the encyclopedia at the foot of it. "Twenty-six-inch remote control?"

"This isn't a hotel. It's a hole in the road."

What Casey said wasn't too far from the truth, but at least it was a small step up from tramping the streets and sleeping rough. I wasn't cut out to be a vagrant.

I stretched out on the bed, which was damp and lumpy, and it sagged so much in the middle that it felt more like a hammock, but after last night I reckon I could have slept then and there if it weren't for Casey; he had begun pacing up and down the room like a caged animal, complaining about how boring the town was and what a dump the hotel turned out to be. I wasn't going to argue with either of those points—the town was boring and the hotel was a dump, but I really don't think that was the reason Casey was so grouchy. It was because he was missing some afternoon drama serial he'd got used to, and to be honest I don't think it would have mattered what state the place was in, if there had been a television in the room I reckon we could just as well have been stuck in a dank underground sewer, with dripping walls and rats under our feet, and I don't think he would have minded a bit.

"You want some music?" I pulled the cassette player from my encyclopedia. I knew it wouldn't be as good as a TV but I figured it might calm him down a little. We'd only been in the room five minutes or so and at this rate he was going to pace a hole right through the carpet. It was like watching a junkie suffering withdrawal symptoms.

"That's a handy book," he said, nodding to the encyclopedia. He sat back onto the bed and stared at the cassette player as if he were going to see something on the machine itself. When the slow movement of Mendelssohn's Fourth began, he almost fell off the edge of the bed.

"I thought you said music."

I launched the nearest thing I could find at him—a pillow. But I understood how he felt. I was the same once. I never gave things a second chance and with music, like other things, that's important. Nobody listens to a record for the first time and thinks it's great. You've got to hear it a few times, then it either grows on you, or it doesn't. Most people don't give things like that the chance, but I don't care. That's not my problem.

I guess I must have fallen asleep listening to the music, because the next thing I knew it was dark, except for a dim red glow, filtering in through the window from a neon sign outside.

I sat up and was trying to adjust my eyes to the situation when something hit me on the chest.

I almost jumped out of my skin. Then I looked across the room and noticed Casey, shadowy red from the neon, sitting on the bed opposite. He was eating something, and I realized that whatever it was, he had thrown a bag to me. It still felt warm through the paper.

It smelled great.

When I'd managed to rip the paper open it turned out to be a burger and fries. Normally I wouldn't touch the fries if they weren't drowned in ketchup, but that night I was more than halfway through the bag before I realized that there wasn't any on them. I must have been starving but that didn't surprise me; it was after eight and the last thing I'd eaten was the chocolate bar I'd shared with Casey, earlier that morning.

I'd just finished the last of the fries—which for some reason I always leave until last, when I noticed something strange. The cassette was still playing softly in the background. The same tape that Casey had made fun of earlier, had been rewound and was quietly replaying. I didn't say anything because I knew he would say something sarcastic like he was planning to try for the Guinness Book of World Records, but I think he was beginning to like it.

The next day I woke really early. Sleeping in a doorway, being out early, and drowsing in the afternoon had screwed up my sleeping habits something rotten. It wasn't much after five and morning hadn't yet broken. I tried everything I could to get back to sleep: counting sheep, pacing the room, the usual things like that. The problem was that I'd only had problems sleeping once before, that was over five years ago when I was having some pretty restless nights. Then, I was given some pills which helped. Without them, I wasn't sure how to deal with it. In the end I gave up trying and just sat on the bed waiting for the dawn.

Casey didn't stir the whole time. It was like he was in some kind of trance. Deep and restful, and I sort of envied him for it. It's funny how people can envy real things like cars and hi-fis and money, and then something as simple as a decent night's sleep just the same.

Casey eventually turned over, still sleeping, and it suddenly struck me that I'd only known him a couple of days. It was strange; looking across that unfamiliar room, it was as if I were looking at someone I'd known my entire life, a person I grew up with, went through school with and shared all the hassles, and the laughs, and the memories that that entails. That's the only way I can describe it really. It's kind of difficult to put into words, and even harder to understand. I guess there are just some people you seem to know the moment you meet them, and then there are others you can know for years and not really know them at all. I felt as if I knew Casey better than anyone I'd known my entire life. Since my parents were killed I've moved around so much I've never really known anyone long enough to get to know them really well. I think it would be nice to do so, someday.

By seven o'clock I was beginning to hate the room, the way Casey had hated it the night before. I began to see things I hadn't noticed before: the peeling paint, the falling plaster, and the damp, musty smell of the blankets which made me feel like I was about to be sick. And it suddenly seemed as if the place were getting smaller.

I decided to get out before the clanking of the water pipes drove me crazy. I'm usually a fairly patient person but when something like that does start to bug me—and

I figure two hours nonstop is enough to bug the hell out of just about anyone—it can really work me up until I'm ready to explode. It's worse when there's nothing you can do about it.

It was cold out, and at that time the streets were practically empty, except for a few people scurrying for buses. Most of the shops hadn't opened yet, but I eventually found an Indian place down one of the grimy side streets. The sign outside referred to the place as a "Fine Authentic Delicatessen" but I guess there must have been a change of ownership since it was painted, because inside it turned out to be nothing more than a seedy back-street grocery. The type of place that sells anything from plastic wastebasket liners to cheap digital watches and second-hand paperbacks. But they did have a bit of Indian stuff—the smell of it was so strong I could hardly breathe and my eyes began to smart. I got the girl behind the counter to warm up two portions of shrimp curry and ordered side servings of rice and nan bread. I figured Casey would be up and ready for breakfast by the time I made it back to the hotel. I hoped he was. The place could be so boring without anyone to talk to, even if a lot of the time it was arguing over whose fault the whole situation was.

Before going back, I took a short detour and stopped at the newsstand we'd bought the chocolate bar from the day before. There I bought the biggest bottle of lemonade I could find. Anyone who's ever tried Indian food will know that curries are practically impossible to eat without it.

I hoped Casey appreciated it. Spicy food isn't everyone's favorite, but I could eat it until it came out of my ears.

Gran always got on to me about my eating habits. But I didn't mind because she didn't really know what she was talking about. Her idea of a fancy meal was to open a tin of salmon and throw it into an omelette.

When I reached the hotel I noticed a car parked near the entrance that hadn't been there earlier, but I didn't think much about it other than how smart it looked. I don't know what make it was. Foreign I guess; and that color described in the trade as ox-blood red.

I made it past the hotel registration desk and was about to move onto the steps leading to our first floor room when I heard a voice call from behind.

"You just missed him."

Turning, I looked at the guy behind the desk.

"What?"

"Your father's just gone up."

I scanned the area. The guy must have been talking to me, there was no one else around.

Your father's gone up, he'd said. I could have told him how and why that was impossible but instead I just shrugged. The hotel had lots of rooms and it was probably easy to make a mistake with so many guests. Besides, the guy looked half gone. I went on up.

When I got to the room we'd rented, the door was locked. I was sure I'd left it open when I went out. Maybe Casey was up, I thought—out, even. I hoped he hadn't gone for breakfast, too. Putting the bottle of lemonade on the floor, I began to search my pockets for the key when I heard a noise from inside.

Casey was in. For some reason I felt relieved about that. Another noise sounded from the room, louder this time and I suddenly had a weird vision of him jogging on the spot or doing some sort of aerobic exercise—you know the sort of touch-your-toes thing they do on morning TV—but I quickly dismissed the thought. Like I said earlier, I reckoned I knew Casey pretty well by then and was fairly sure he wasn't the sweatpants-and-running-shoes type. The only running I could ever imagine Casey doing was away from trouble. That was easy to picture.

I tried the handle again. The door was definitely locked.

I thought back to when I'd left the room and the harder I thought about it the more sure I was. The door had been unlocked.

I moved close and held my ear to the wood. The noise seemed to have stopped.

Total silence.

Then an almighty crash of something hard and brittle like a glass or plate, slamming against the wall.

I couldn't find the keys.

"Casey?"

There was no reply and the noise inside was getting louder—moving closer. I thought I heard someone cry out and I still had no idea what was going on. I suppose it sounds naive now, but even after everything that had gone before, I never dreamed I'd walk through the door and see Casey fighting for his life with some fellow I'd never seen before.

It was only when I heard the gunshot that everything pulled together. The car. The guy at the front desk. The noise of a struggle and the gunshot.

The gunshot! The noise of it ripped through my head.

The take-out bag dropped from my hands as my legs

went to rubber and I felt like something hot had just exploded in my gut.

"CASEY?" I pounded on the door for what seemed like ages. It never even crossed my mind that whoever it was who fired the shot, was still inside with a loaded gun. I just kept hitting the door and pulling on the handle. Shouting. "Open the door!"

There still was no reply and a thousand thoughts hit my mind at once. I thought of running down to the front desk to get a passkey, about kicking the door down, of calling the cops. Then I remembered I still had the key on me and as I began to fumble clumsily through my pockets, the door cracked open.

All I noticed was the blood. It was as if my eyes couldn't focus on anything else but the red oozing over the white of the shirt. It was like being under a hypnotic spell. I didn't even know it was Casey at first, his face was so twisted with pain and drained of color.

I don't remember doing it, but somehow I managed to step into the room. I felt in a worse state than Casey. I couldn't stop shaking and for a minute my head suddenly went light and I thought I was going to pass out.

"He's dead," I heard Casey say. His voice sounded so calm and controlled. I hadn't noticed the body until I almost fell over it. My mind still wasn't in gear.

"What happened?" I heard a strange voice say and realized that it belonged to me.

"I don't know, Jim. He just came at me. I think I've been shot."

My stomach heaved. It's something you hear all the time on TV but when someone in a show says it you know it's not real. You don't think anything about it, just sit back and wait for the next scene. But in real life, when you hear someone you know say it, it hits you like a kick in the teeth. I suppose watching those TV shows came in handy though because, not really knowing why, I pulled the thin under-blanket from the bed and began tearing it to shreds, then folding a large square of it into a soft pad, I gently pressed it onto Casey's arm and told him to hold it there until I got a doctor. If I hadn't seen someone on television do it, I don't know what I would have done. I was moving to the door when Casey pulled on my arm.

"No!"

I turned and looked at him as if I hadn't heard right.

"No doctor!" he gasped.

"But you've been shot! You've got to . . ."

"It's not that bad." He rushed out the words and noticing my horrified, worried expression added through clenched teeth, "It went clear through."

I didn't think that made much difference.

"You need attention," I told him firmly. He sank wearily onto the edge of the bed and nodded to the unmoving figure at the foot of it: the man's chest was soaked with a glistening liquid, which because the shirt was black and the body lay in the gray shadow of the bed, could have been water—anything, but I knew it was blood. Casey's knife lay beside him, in a wedge of light that cut through a gap in the curtains, and the blade shone red.

"What about *him?*" Casey sighed. "You bring a doctor here and we're both going to get a lot more attention than we can handle."

I don't know why but I suddenly felt the urge to laugh. Maybe it was because I didn't know what else to do. It was a strange feeling because I also wanted to cry and scream at the same time.

Finally I didn't do any of those things, but found myself searching through the pockets of the man by the bed. It didn't bother me that he was dead, because everything had become so unreal, like I suddenly realized it was all part of some terrible dream that I'd wake from any minute, and find myself back in my old cluttered room at Gran's place.

My warm, safe, secure room back home . . .

I found what I had been searching for in the inside pocket of the dead man's jacket, and as I pulled the set of keys out, the back of my hand brushed against the warm, sticky liquid which had soaked into the cloth.

Casey stood. He looked at me calmly and said he thought he could walk. I could hardly believe it. He'd just been shot at close range and he was in more control than I was. I couldn't stop my hands from shaking and wished I were someplace else. Anyplace else.

We made it along the corridor to the stairs OK. Casey, with my old blazer draped over his shoulders so the blood couldn't be seen, was leaning against me, but trying not to show it. We had to take the stairs because like everything else in that dump of a hotel, the elevator wasn't working. It was hard because the stairway was steep and narrow, and I was trying not to make any sudden movements that would jolt Casey—I had the feeling he was hurt worse than he was making out. It took us about three minutes to reach the bottom of the stairway, which in ordinary circumstances couldn't have taken us much more than thirty seconds.

But we both knew that the circumstances were anything

but ordinary and I was just thankful when we reached the bottom without either of us falling or passing out cold.

The moment we stepped into the lobby, I could see the guy at the reception desk staring at us. He watched silently for a moment but I knew he was going to say something.

"Hey! What the hell is going on up there?"

We didn't stop moving. I thought that if we did, it might be difficult to get started again. I just kept staring at the glass exit doors and continued in that direction. I could see the street clearly outside, but it was like looking at it from a vast distance—it seemed so far away, as if the lobby had expanded to ten times its original size.

"Hey!"

It was the man again. I suddenly had the awful feeling he was going to run out, grab my arm, and pull us both back. I didn't know anything about the guy and I realized I hated him. Hated him more than I had hated anyone in my entire life.

Then I remembered his question. "What's going on up there?"

Without stopping, I turned my head sharply towards him.

"You tell me," I yelled. "It's those jerks on the second floor. They kept us awake half the night. You should do something about them before someone complains."

My hatred must have sounded in my voice. I sounded so angry that the guy just stood there openmouthed as we pushed our way through the glass doors.

Stepping out onto the street was like moving from a hot, sticky room, into a cool, refreshing breeze that blew away my anger. I didn't hate the guy any longer.

The car was still there. Just to the left of the exit doors. Its polished surface gleamed in the morning sun. The color was ox-blood. I was sure of it now. It made my stomach turn.

We stopped as soon as we were out of sight of the registration desk. We both needed to rest, but also because there was one other person on the street and I figured it would be best to wait until the area was completely clear before going for the car. I thought it would look pretty suspicious Casey and me letting ourselves into a smart-looking rig like that.

"Can you drive it?" Casey asked as I helped him into the passenger seat once the street became clear.

"I drove a milk truck once," I told him. That had been during the last few months I spent with Jack and Ellie. I'd talked my way into a job delivering milk. Mondays to Fridays—five-thirty to seven. The money wasn't bad but like I said before, I'm not too hot in the mornings so I only stuck with it for a month. I was just the delivery boy but sometimes, if I pressed hard enough, I could talk the guy who owned the truck (and I mean real truck. The route was rural and far too big to tool around in one of those dinky little Matchbox toy things you see in small towns.) into letting me drive around the quieter parts of the area. I've always been good at persuasion. It's a handy talent which I suppose I got from my parents. Dad once told me that the role of an actor was to lead an audience. To work and manipulate it in the way a potter works an ordinary piece of clay into something infinitely more beautiful. In the theater you do it for the audience. In life you do it for your own benefit. But either way, the technique and the challenge is pretty much the same.

The old milk truck had taught me the basic mechanics of driving. How the gears were arranged and which foot pedals were which, but this car had little in common with that beat-up old clunker. The foot pedals were the same but that's about all. The dash was much more complex than the basic speedometer and fuel gauge I'd gotten used to, it was like moving from an ancient biplane into the mind-blowing fuselage of a modern 747. I even had trouble finding where to insert the ignition key. That took a minute or so, and it was no relief when it eventually turned because all the gauges suddenly sprang to life, and little windows which I hadn't noticed before lit up orange and green and began to flash weird-looking symbols everywhere.

For a while I just sat there and stared. Like a rabbit caught in the glare of an approaching truck. Then Casey shuddered beside me which broke the spell and I did the only thing I could: I looked over the dash to the street ahead and turned the key again.

The engine fired on the first try and a moment later all the lights from the little windows and gauge began to fade. I suddenly realized that the car wasn't as different from the milk truck as I first thought. It seemed like most of the gauges and things were just there to make the car look flashy. I figured they weren't really necessary and tried not to think about them.

After that I got us moving fairly quickly but I was still glad there weren't any cops about because it started pretty jumpily, and as we turned off the quiet road and onto High Street I think it drew a lot of attention to us. People just stopped and stared at us as if they had nothing better to do. I didn't find it too difficult to ignore them, though.

By the time we'd moved out of the main town area onto the quieter, straighter roads which ran through the smart, tree-lined residential areas, I figured I was beginning to handle the car fairly well and wondered what Casey thought of my driving. As I looked across, I almost swerved into a lamppost. Casey was slumped down in the seat and his eyes were closed. He reminded me of the guy we'd left back at the hotel.

"Case?" I shrieked as I straightened up the car.

I thought he was dying.

Groaning at the sharp sound in my voice he muttered in a grumbling, I've-been-disturbed voice. "What?"

I shook my head sheepishly. "Nothing."

After several minutes of silent driving, I glanced quickly across again. This time keeping a firm hold on the steering wheel. Casey really looked awful. His face was still pale and his hair—soaked in sweat—was caked across his forehead.

I felt almost as lousy as he looked because I didn't know what to do. In the end I just said what I was thinking.

"Oh Christ, Casey! I don't know how to handle this. You should see a doctor."

"No, Jim." He hardly moved as he spoke and his eyes remained closed.

"Well, what?" I slapped the wheel in frustration. "You're practically bleeding to death in front of me and I don't even have a Band-Aid."

He looked up sleepily and tried his best to give an encouraging grin. "If you're trying to reassure me, Taylor, you're doing a terrific job. You wanna order the coffin now or are you planning to keep me on ice until the January sales?"

"I'm sorry. I'm just nervous," I said. "I've never been in a situation like this before."

"Really?" he asked with quiet surprise, then added, "Hell, I get shot all the time."

It was probably the best thing he could have said to ease my mind. He was getting back to his usual sarcastic self, so maybe he wasn't hurt as bad as I thought; his mind was working OK.

"Stop at the next town. Get some bandages and aspirin."

"Does it hurt bad?" I asked, glancing at him again. I still wasn't sure how much he was holding back.

"YESSS . . ." he shrieked and I jumped a little. Then he looked as if he regretted it, like he was sorry he'd shouted at me.

"It's not that bad, Jim." He sighed at my concerned expression. "Just keep your eyes on the road."

I was on the wrong side again, but luckily there was nothing coming from the other direction. I quickly repositioned the car and in an attempt to take my mind off the situation, began thinking how easy driving was, once you got the hang of it, when you didn't have anyone who thinks they know it all breathing down your neck and watching every little movement. Casey made a good passenger.

After almost twenty minutes of driving, we reached a small neighborhood shopping center. There were a lot of expensive cars about. They were all parked on a double yellow line, a no-parking area, and there would have been plenty of room to squeeze the car in with them, but I drove around the area until I found a legitimate parking space just a few minutes' walk from the center. With the flashy car I was driving, and Casey looking like a fugitive from a chain gang, I figured we could get more than enough attention without advertising for any more.

We must have stopped on the rich side of town because all the shops were really smart. They all had those flashy, digital cash registers that play a tune when the buttons are pressed, and the girls who operated them looked classy and attractive in their smart shop uniforms. Every town I've ever been to has been the same. They all have a rich side where the people live in fancy houses, drive big expensive cars and couldn't care less about the people living on the other side. I suppose it's the same all over. Most of the shops down our way are old and dumpy. They use cash registers that wouldn't look out of place in a Dickens' novel and most of the salesclerks would make good last-minute stand-ins for the opening scene of *Macbeth*. But at least the stuff they sell is cheaper. I spent almost fifteen pounds on groceries that I reckon back home wouldn't have cost us much more than ten.

Casey was almost asleep when I got back to the car, but when I got in and pulled the door shut, he sat up and looked at me a little dazed.

"Here," I said pulling the ring from a can of Coke and handing it to him with two aspirin from a small bottle I'd bought. He swallowed them silently and washed them down with the Coke. As he handed the can back he frowned.

"I prefer Dr. Pepper," he explained.

"OK." I grinned. I was feeling a lot easier now that we were away from the hotel. "Next time you get shot and need something to wash down the painkillers, I'll have a crate of Dr. Pepper standing by."

"Thanks, Taylor." He yawned then snuggled down into the seat and closed his eyes again. I'd planned to finish the Coke before starting off again, but some guy who'd parked in front of us suddenly appeared and began piling shopping bags into his hatchback, at the insistence of a fat, bossy woman I figured was his wife. When the guy noticed us, he gave a long hard stare that at other times might have caused me to shout out something like, *Who the hell do you think you're looking at, Jack?* I sometimes wish I had more control over my mouth. It's got me into big trouble more than a few times. This time, though, I just decided to get out of the area as soon as possible, so I dropped the unfinished can out the window and pulled away as smoothly as I could.

After a few miles we turned onto a one-way highway, which I decided is the best kind of road to travel on: straight and wide with no sharp turns or oncoming traffic to bother about. It was a seventy-miles-per-hour limit but I kept to a steady fifty because I wasn't in any great hurry to get to where I was heading, and I remembered an article I'd read in *Popular Mechanics,* which said that cars burn up a lot more gas once they go over the fifty-five mark. Gas isn't cheap and I figured we needed all the money we had, without burning it up in exhaust fumes.

We were in the country now. The green and brown fields stretched as far as the eye could see.

There was the smell of the country, too.

I'm not sure if it's the same with other people, but sometimes, when I smell something that I haven't come across in years, it can remind me of the time and place I'd last encountered it, more vividly and accurately than any photo or diary could. It's a bit unnerving, but I think it might be the same with other people. I decided to ask Casey about it when we stopped. I closed the window to shut the smell out, but it still managed to filter its way in.

We were getting closer, I could tell that, though I'm not sure how. It wasn't just the smell. Maybe it was the way the trees in the distance were grouped, or the vaguely familiar way the little red farm buildings were dotted across the landscape. It was hard to tell; my memory's not too good on certain subjects, and it had been a long time since I'd been this far north. A lot had happened since then.

Then I saw the sign which confirmed everything.

Malton. Turnoff. One mile to the left.

It's amazing how six simple letters, arranged on a plain, ordinary-looking road sign can have such a powerful effect. Most would have read it without a second glance. I almost ran the car off the highway and after straightening up, had to fight a very real urge to slam on the brakes and make a sharp U-turn. But as the car rocked, Casey stirred. He didn't wake up, just turned restlessly and drifted back into sleep, and he reminded me what I was doing here. Why I was driving toward a place I once swore I'd never return to: Casey needed my help and I knew I couldn't turn my back on him, just because a part of me was afraid some ghost from the past would tap me on the shoulder, and remind me of how things were not so long ago. Of how wonderful everything had been, and how by comparison, everything since had become cold and empty.

I continued on. Trying to convince myself that perhaps

it was even better that way: not having anyone left to care about. It should give a person the freedom to do whatever he chose, not force him into a dark corner that's impossible to get out of. I was thinking about this when we reached the turnoff. It came up much sooner than I'd expected. One minute I was cruising along the clear highway and then all of a sudden, there it was, like it had appeared out of thin air. I suppose it was because my mind hadn't been entirely on the road.

It wasn't long before we were driving along the narrow dirt road which ran to the house, and continued on to the town another mile or so beyond. As we traveled closer the car began to pick up speed, though I didn't realize it until we came to a sharp bend and almost lost control and ran into the ditch. Luckily we just scratched the paint against the hard branches of the hawthorn bushes which edged the road. Casey didn't even stir.

I suppose I'd been driving faster because I wanted to get it over with. That's just the way I am. If there's something I don't want to do, and can think of a way to get out of it, I will—but if there's no way I can, I'd as soon get it over than spend ages fretting about it.

In the end it turned out nowhere near as bad as I'd expected, seeing the house again. When it first came into view as the road turned towards it, I felt a little funny but that feeling soon passed as we moved closer, and when we turned off the road into the yard it was just like looking at any other old run-down farmhouse. Just an ordinary-looking place with a plain concrete yard and a few crumbling, red brick outbuildings, surrounded by a rotting off-white fence.

It's hard to describe what a relief it was to see it again and not feel the urge to turn and run.

It was exactly how it had looked the last time I'd been there. Nothing had changed. Everything was in its proper place and yet in some way it was different, but not because it had aged over the years and become worn by the weather. It was my view of it that had altered. The last time I'd seen it, it was through the eyes of a nine-year-old boy. Then it was like an enchanted castle: unique, stately, and grand. Now, for the first time in my life I was seeing it for what it was—a small weather-beaten old farmhouse, just like any one of the dozens of others that covered the area.

I switched off the ignition and sat for a moment clutching the wheel, silently looking the place over as I listened to the comforting sound of Casey's quiet breathing.

I was about to tap him on the shoulder and tell him we were here when I caught sight of my jacket still draped over his shoulders; at the arm, the color was darker where the blood had soaked through. He now looked so peaceful after the ordeal at the hotel, I couldn't bring myself to wake him—and thinking about it, I didn't see any real reason why I should. I decided to leave him to sleep while I took a look around the house for myself.

The door at the front of the house was either locked or jammed, and all the windows looked like they were securely fastened. There was a small pane of glass right next to the front door which I could have easily shattered, and then reached the inside lock. No one would hear and I don't think it would have mattered anyway because the place had been deserted for so long, but still for some reason I couldn't bring myself to smash it. I think it might have been because, even after all the years away from the place, I still thought of it as "our house," and still felt a kind of responsibility towards it.

Actually, the house was never really ours—even in the old days. My parents just leased the place on a yearly basis when the former tenants couldn't afford its upkeep any longer. I think the guy who actually owns it is some sort of aristocrat. A lord or baron who, according to Gran, only bought it in the first place as some kind of tax scam. He owns a lot of the houses around that area and I guess he must think ours is just as derelict as some of the others, because it wasn't rented again when our lease ran out five years ago. Even then it was fairly run-down. Dad always planned to fix it up. He even set up a workshop in the yard, but to be honest, he wasn't much of a handyman. I guess it's just that people are rarely good at more than one thing, and Dad was an actor, whether he liked it or not. He could walk onto a bare stage with a hammer and chisel and play the greatest carpenter who ever lived, but that's as far as it went. Personally, I preferred it that way.

I circled the yard to the other side. The back door was locked, too. I think it was Uncle Jack who locked up for the last time. He was a Scout leader and always did things correctly. Methodically. By the book. All the back windows were shut securely too—he probably even watered the plants.

Like all the woodwork on the house, the frame around the door hadn't been painted in years and most of the existing paint had begun to flake, leaving the woodwork beneath open to rot. With one good shove, the frame splintered and the door swung open. As I stepped into the tiny, whitewashed porch, I promised my conscience that I'd fix it as soon as I could.

My footsteps echoed on the floor tiles when I stepped into the kitchen, and I vaguely remembered that happening before. Something to do with new shoes and someone complaining about the noise they made. This time the noise was made greater by the fact that most of the furniture had been removed from the room. In fact, apart from the stove and built-in cabinets, the only other thing was a wooden chair, and that had probably been left because one of its legs was shorter than the rest, and it always rocked when you sat on it. I remembered that clearly and wondered how many more memories the place would conjure.

I left the kitchen just as a tune began playing in my head. I think it's called *Green, Green Grass of Home*. It was one of my mother's favorites. She sang it all the time. I used to like it then, but now every time I hear it, I switch off the radio or leave the room. Thankfully, it doesn't come on very often.

The living room wasn't as bare as the kitchen. I was glad about that. At least we'd have somewhere to sit. Whoever it was that cleared out after the crash obviously didn't like the couch we had, because that was the only thing they'd left, apart from the piano, which they probably couldn't have carried even if they wanted to. I tried it.

It was a little out of tune, but not that bad, considering it had been left for almost six years. But then it was a very good make. It was the only thing Mum insisted on when they decided to move out here. She was a really good player and had started teaching me. I haven't played since but I could still tap out a tune from memory. It's one of those things you don't forget. Like the name of your first junior-high homeroom teacher. It'll probably be there for life.

I sank onto the sofa and stretched out, surprised at how small it was. My legs reached over the end of it now. It was only a small love seat, but I remember sleeping on it when I stayed up to watch the late night films on TV and it dwarfed me then. I was drifting to sleep with that comfortable memory in my head when the door swung open.

"Hey, Jim!"

My heart missed a beat and I immediately sat up. It was only Casey. Of course. I don't know who else I was expecting it to be . . . But Casey's voice could sometimes be quite deep, and just for a second it sounded a little like . . .

I shook my head and looked around, disoriented. I wondered if I'd been asleep or not. My watch had stopped at 8:24 A.M.

"Where the hell are we?" Casey shuffled into the room and sank into the armchair in front of the empty fireplace.

"The country."

"Yeah?" He looked impressed and began to scan the room with interest. When he turned his head to look out of the uncurtained window on his left, the side where he'd been wounded, he winced slightly.

"How're you feeling now?" I asked. He still didn't look too good.

"Not bad considering I've been hit point-blank with a howitzer," he pointed out, then shook his head with a bit of a smile and confessed that he'd come out of some street fights feeling worse. That might have been true. I've been in a few fights myself where I've finished up feeling like I've been shot in about ten different places. Though I can never remember feeling anything at the time—which I suppose is strange, I think it's something to do with all the adrenalin that gets pumped around when you're in there.

I seem to get into a lot of fights. God knows why. I've never started one in my life. It's just that I find it hard to walk away from a situation once something has started, and when you've traveled around as much as I have, you get into quite a lot of situations. There's always some jerk who wants to see what the new kid's made of. Most of them are all mouth and carry around a tough reputation that's totally false. There are a lot of people like that about. People who are really tough don't need to boast about it.

"Hell, it's cold in here." Casey shuddered. I didn't think it was too bad, but Casey was shaking like he was freezing, and sweat had started to pour down his face. I was just beginning to think he was doing OK and now he looked almost as bad as he had back at the hotel. Perhaps it was a delayed reaction to everything that had happened. I'd thought he was acting too calm at the time.

I started a fire going with some scrap wood I knew I'd find in one of the outbuildings at the back of the house. It was an old shed my dad had converted into a workshop when we first moved here. There was always wood stacked in the corners.

I moved Casey's chair closer to the hearth and when the fire was roaring, went out to the car and brought in the box of groceries I'd bought earlier. After shopping in the supermarket, I'd stopped at the drugstore and bought a box of sterile dressings and I reckoned now was the time to use them. Casey eyed them suspiciously as I pulled them from the box. "What's that?"

"Bandages. We've got to do up that arm."

"It doesn't feel that bad now. Can't we just leave it and see what happens?"

He didn't speak with much conviction, but I did.

"No way," I said positively. "You want to get gangrene?"

He was thinking about it when I moved over and began to ease my jacket away from his shoulders, starting with the right side and taking it slower as I worked around to the wounded side. The blood that had soaked through the cloth had dried and it cracked as I eased the cloth away. For a second, there was a brief resistance as the blood pulled at the skin and flaked away, causing Casey to groan a little. When I pulled the coat clean away and saw the arm, I groaned, too. I wasn't expecting roses but what I saw made me sick. The entire arm of his white shirt had turned dark purple with blood which had dried and hardened like solid black plaster. At the front of the arm was a small hole cut into the cloth and around it, a circle of dark red blood had foamed up and solidified. At the opposite side of the arm, both cloth and skin had splayed out from the impact of the bullet. Casey just stared at it with a kind of morbid fascination.

"Don't look too good, does it?"

"Probably looks worse than it is," I told him hopefully, and trusted I was right. I didn't know too much about medicine, but I knew that I wouldn't be able to do anything until I got that shirt off and I wouldn't be able to do that without a pair of scissors.

Moving back into the kitchen I began to search through the drawers and cupboards of the few fitted cabinets that were there. I returned to the living room a few minutes later without finding any scissors, but I did come across a pair of old pruning shears in a toolbox I found in the outhouse. When Casey caught sight of them he looked at me as if I were crazy. He knew what I was thinking.

"You're not coming near me with them."

"Come on, Case, we've got to get that shirt off. Here, hold this." I handed him a small bottle of antiseptic and, pulling a different bottle from my pocket, unscrewed the top and swapped it with the one he held.

"Drink some of this!"

Casey sniffed at the liquid warily. "What is it?"

"Whiskey. I found it in the kitchen while I was looking for the scissors."

"I hate it," he told me with real disgust in his voice, but he didn't hand back the bottle.

"OK. But this might hurt," I said as I surveyed the mess, deciding how and where to start. I eventually chose to cut from the cuff upwards. Even with the strong pruners, the shirt wasn't easy to get through. The blood had dried it hard as sheet metal.

"You know how much that shirt cost?" Casey grumbled as I moved further up the arm, cutting the shirt away as gently as I could. At one point he flinched a little, and letting out a quiet, stifled groan, took a drink from the bottle I'd handed him.

I cut away the entire sleeve of the shirt to about an inch above the elbow. That had been difficult enough but I knew the next bit was going to be a lot harder. Especially for Casey. The rest of his shirt had caked hard onto the ragged skin and somehow it had to be pulled away. I soaked the arm until it was saturated and dripping with antiseptic and that loosened the shirt a little, but it was still sticking. Slowly and carefully, I began to peel the cloth away as best I could. It was a horrible feeling, like I was peeling an actual layer of skin away, and it must have hurt like hell, but Casey didn't say much. His teeth were clenched and his hands were white, one from gripping the arm of the chair, the other clenched tight around the whisky bottle from which he had begun taking increasingly frequent gulps. I don't know how long it took to clear all the shirt away, then clean the wound and dress it, but by the time I had, I was sweating like a dog and Casey was pretty well soused. He kept saying things like, "Knew you could do it, Jimmy ol' pal" and "Who needs surgeons with a buddy like you?"

"Yeah. Well, don't blame me when it turns bright green and withers to a stump," I warned him and took a drink from the bottle myself. I thought I'd earned it. Casey looked on with a glazed look in his eyes. "Hey, don't drink it all," he mumbled possessively only moments before drifting into a deep sleep.

Getting his denim jacket from the car, I spread it over him with my jacket on top. Then after stoking the fire up and putting a bit more wood on—not so much for it to be dangerous, but enough to keep it going—I went back to the car and tried to find a local station on the radio. I wanted to set my watch, but more than that—though I didn't want to admit it to myself—I wanted to hear the news to see if it mentioned anything about the incident—hell, I still couldn't say *murder*—at the hotel. I'd spent the last few hours trying to convince myself that it really hadn't been that bad, and just maybe the guy hadn't been dead. I know it looked bad, but even a busted nose can bleed pretty bad if you let it. *Yeah, that was true enough,* my conscience invaded my thoughts, *but you don't just let it bleed. You do something about it, not simply lie rigid, staring at the ceiling with eyes wide and dilated.*

The news came on. The reception was bad and I didn't catch the time but I was sure there was no mention of any incident at one of the nearby hotels. Perhaps the story hadn't leaked out yet or was being withheld by the cops until investigations were completed.

Maybe . . . What if . . .

A thousand thoughts churned around in my head, all of them unwanted and I wished I didn't have such an active imagination. I was exhausted and wanted to sleep so badly, but I could see the traffic from the road way off in the distance, and every car that passed seemed to carry with it a wailing, two-tone siren.

I was sure they'd find us.

The next few hours were the longest I've ever spent. There was no way I could sleep. My body was exhausted but my mind was still in overdrive. I left the radio on just to have something to distract my thoughts. Sometimes it helped. Every thirty minutes the news came on, but the only local incidents were a train derailment about fifteen miles away and reports of a visit by some politician I'd never heard of. I did get the time, though. It had just turned twelve when it began to rain and I couldn't stop myself from laughing. I didn't find it funny, just impossibly weird.

If anyone had told me, only a matter of days ago, that I'd be sitting in the yard of our old house in a stolen car, listening to the radio for news of a murder, I would have staked my life on the fact that it could never be true. Anyone would.

It's hard to realize how thin the line between ordinary person and criminal outcast is, and how incredibly easy it is to cross it.

I fell asleep listening to the rhythmic sound of rain gently rattling on the roof of the car.

Crackle and static from the radio woke me. It was 8:20 A.M. and although the sky was cloudy, the morning light was still glaring when I opened my eyes for the first time. But I wasn't complaining. Things always seem better in the light of day.

It was cold outside, so as soon as I got into the house, I went to the kitchen and tried to get the stove working. Because the house was out of the town area, there wasn't a piped-in gas supply. I suppose if there was, it would have been cut off years ago. Instead the stove ran off a big gas cylinder which was kept in a small cupboard next to the sink. It took me ages to refix the line—which Scoutmaster Jack must have disconnected the day he locked up—partly because my hands were cold and fumbly and partly because the only wrench I could find—in a dusty corner of Dad's old workshop—was too big and rusty and kept slipping off the joining nut.

By the time I eventually got the gas lit, my right hand

was raw from rapping against the rough surface of the metal cylinder, and Casey had just staggered into the kitchen.

"Finally came around, eh? You drunken bum," I said as I lit the gas burner and put the only pan there was on to boil.

"No thanks to you," he grumbled. It seemed like every time I saw Casey, he looked awful. This time I didn't feel so bad about it though; it was only a hangover.

"Whydja have to feed me that junk for anyway? I told you I hated whiskey."

"That's not the impression you gave yesterday."

He didn't reply. Just scratched his head, causing his hair to stand out in thick matted peaks, as he dropped into the chair by the stove.

When the water in the pan boiled, I made coffee from a jar of instant and added some powdered milk I'd bought at the supermarket. We had to take turns drinking because there was only one cup. It was chipped and the handle was missing but it was the best I could do. The only other thing I could find was an eggcup.

As the day wore on, Casey began to look better, especially after we had eaten. It was only peanut butter on toast; that was the only thing I'd bought that could be eaten without knives or forks—I suppose I was in a bit of a daze when I was shopping, and all the lights and noise made it difficult to think straight at the time. Now I figured if we were planning to stay much longer we'd have to drive into town and get some cutlery—spreading peanut butter over dry toast with your fingers is pretty disgusting, even if Casey found it fun. By suppertime, even he admitted the novelty had worn off a little. It didn't surprise me. I can't imagine anyone eating a whole family-sized jar of crunchy peanut butter without losing a little enthusiasm for the stuff.

I don't know what it is about the countryside that's special. Back in town, whenever I wake up, I usually have to drag myself out of bed at the last possible moment and then I spend most of what's left of the morning staggering around in a sort of lethargic stupor. Out at the house, though, I hardly ever slept later than eight, which I reckon back at Gran's would have been enough to have her calling the doctor. Half an hour earlier and it might well have been in the local newspaper. I could picture the headline:

TAYLOR UP BEFORE EIGHT—READ ALL ABOUT IT!

The next day I woke early and when Casey appeared about an hour later and said he was feeling OK, we drove into town and spent most of the money we had left on things we thought we would need if we were going to stay at the house a while. We both kind of got carried away in the supermarket and never really stopped to look at the prices, just kept throwing things into the shopping cart while I maneuvered it around the shelves. It's kind of fun if you've never done it before but I think that must wear off after a while—no one else in the store seemed to be enjoying the task.

When the girl at the checkout said "Twenty-seven sixty-four," I nearly had a heart attack and for a moment wondered where on earth I could get that kind of money from. I've just never had that much to spend before and it came as a bit of a shock. Last year I felt like a big spender when

I forked over ten-fifty for an early Beatles double album.

Casey handed me the wallet and I paid the bill. It didn't leave us with much change but I was just relieved there had been enough to cover it.

When we got back, we treated ourselves to the first decent meal we'd had since the whole thing began. It was one of those dried sweet-and-sour dishes that you boil and serve with the rice that's included in the package. The box was described as family-sized and boasted "four large portions" but we decided to make it all anyway and managed to wolf it down without much trouble. It took about thirty hectic minutes to prepare—with Casey anxiously fussing and fretting over the pan like a nervous father awaiting the birth of his first child. Eating it took a lot less time and effort, and clearing away was quicker still: paper plates, which Casey burned in the grate.

After we'd finished cleaning up, Casey pulled from his jacket pocket a small blue box about two inches square. There was a sticker on the side with the name of the store we'd shopped at but I couldn't remember buying it. I didn't even know what it was. The sticker said six ninety-nine but I didn't bother checking the receipt because I didn't think it would be on it. I figured Casey had slipped it into his pocket while I was busy playing Mario Andretti with the shopping cart.

"I think it's some sort of game." He held the box close to his ear and shook it as if it would give him a clue to its contents. It didn't.

He shrugged. "I thought it might help us pass the time. I know it's nothing special but it's the best I could do. It's kinda hard to get a portable TV under your coat without it looking suspicious."

He had opened the box before I had a chance to ask if he was serious.

It was a game. One of those complicated strategy ones where you have a selection of cards with different symbols and numbers on them, the idea being to match your cards with your opponents and build up a score from the numbers on them.

Like Casey said, it didn't seem like anything special but it became quite addictive after a while. That day we played right up until the sunset turned the sky a warm orange-red and tinted the white of the cards we were playing with pink.

I won that time, but as the days passed that began to change. People who didn't know him well might have gotten the impression that Casey wasn't too bright. This wasn't true. I'm not saying he was an academic genius, but in his own way he was smarter than most; always quick to pick up things and good at thinking things through. In the end, when we were both getting tired of the game I got the impression he was letting me win the odd round just so I wouldn't feel bad.

The first few days at the house were a bit disorganized and awkward, but by the fifth day we were beginning to settle in and develop routines which made the stay easier: Casey found he had a knack for cooking so he did most of that, and I set about making the place a little more comfortable and tidy. The way I remembered it.

To pass the time in the evenings I taught Casey how to play "Yesterday" on the piano, and he showed me how to use his picklocks to open every door and window in the house. He was looking a lot better by then and I was so relieved his arm hadn't withered away to a stump.

I'd almost forgotten about the man at the hotel. It was like it had happened years ago. Or not at all. Time has that effect; you can forget about almost anything if you give it long enough, and I was really beginning to believe that the whole thing had been brushed aside and forgotten.

Sometimes I can be really stupid.

By the time we had been at the house a week, I was getting sick of all the peanut butter dishes Casey had been concocting, and he was growing restless, so I decided to deal with all the problems together and suggested we go fishing; even if we didn't catch anything it would make a change from hanging around the house. The stream wasn't far—no more than a mile. I remembered where it was from all the times I had been with my dad. We'd caught some pretty respectable fish there.

Casey got really excited about going. No one had taken him fishing before. But I warned him before we went that I didn't think we'd catch much because it was difficult enough with decent tackle, but with worms dangling from a couple of bent pins it would be virtually impossible. I might as well have saved my breath, though, because he went there convinced we'd clear the stream. We didn't. I never even got a bite and all Casey got was a young bullhead which he decided to throw back because it was so small and neither of us wanted to gut it. I didn't even know how. My dad always cleaned the ones I caught because I couldn't stand to cut them open.

Still, it hadn't been a bad day. The weather was good. It was probably the last really good day of summer and it was nice just to sit by the stream, talking quietly, or leaning back listening to the relaxing sounds of the countryside. Somewhere not far away a farm tractor was ploughing or threshing, and further away came the sound of blasting from the old granite quarry, just as I remembered it. Maybe I was wrong. Perhaps some things never change.

Mum and Dad never thought much of that quarry, but I kind of liked the sounds that came from the site. Maybe it was because it had always been there, so to me they were as much a part of our life in the country as the stream and the tractors and the crows in the morning. Mum finally explained to me that it reminded them too much of the city and pointed out that they moved to the country to get away from the noise. Eventually we got into the routine of staying around the house most of the week while we stocked up with cakes and fruit juice and homemade pastries, preparing for a massive picnic in the fields each fine Sunday afternoon. That was the only day you could be sure they wouldn't be blasting the granite.

I'd forgotten about the quarry until I heard the first dull explosion, then the memory of it came rushing back. If I closed my eyes I could have been nine years old again, sitting on the riverbank with my parents beside me: Dad would be lying across the red-checked tablecloth which was spread over the grass like a big regal carpet, while Mum unloaded our old wicker picnic basket as she laughed quietly at some joke he had just cracked. And me, I'd be sitting easy on the bank, carving an arrow from a fallen branch with my prized penknife which is now just a rusty ghost of its former self; then it was like a great magical saber, big enough and strong enough to protect me from any danger I could have faced. But then it seemed as if the only danger I faced was maybe getting stung while trying to catch bees in a pickle jar, and the only problem I had was how to tell Mum I'd spilled maple syrup on the living room carpet.

The wind rustled the tall river reeds by the water and, yeah, I could have been nine years old all over again with my parents beside me, except for one small difference. When they heard the old granite quarry being mined for the first time they didn't jump up and shriek, "Jesus Christ, Jim! What the hell was that?"

I explained about the quarry as we were walking back to the house. Casey asked me how I knew about it and I just said we passed it when we first drove here. I don't know why I hadn't told him about the house yet, because I could tell Casey anything. I guess I don't like being asked about my past too much. As far as Casey knew, the house was just a place I came across while we were heading out of town. I eventually told him about it, though—two days later.

It was just after one o'clock and we were in the living room eating the last pack of sweet-and-sour boil-a-meal we had left. The day had started off wet and overcast, but by midday the sky had cleared and the fields were bathed in the rich golden sunlight we were growing accustomed to.

"I didn't realize how pretty the countryside could be," Casey remarked, quietly—to himself as much as me. He was looking out of the window like he'd been doing a lot lately. He had even repositioned his chair for a better view over the fields to the south, where you could see the church spire peeking over the trees from the town way off in the distance.

"You should see it in the spring," I whispered. "It's at its best then. The trees are so fresh and bright, and the grass so crisp and new, when the sun shines in the mornings it's like looking out over a sea of brilliant emerald green."

Casey didn't say anything, but I could tell by the expression that crossed his face that he didn't believe what I had just told him—and I had got to know him well enough to know that he wouldn't until I proved it. So I led him upstairs to my old bedroom.

I got him to sit on the bed and he watched curiously as I started to peel away the blue wallpaper from a spot opposite the window. That was easy to do because the walls were so damp, the strips came away whole. The first piece revealed behind it the letters OOM. Blue paint over yellowing plaster.

"What is that?" Casey fidgeted anxiously and his eyes grew wide like he was watching some kind of conjuring trick. The next strip revealed it. Across the wall in kingfisher blue was the statement: JIM'S ROOM.

When we first moved to the house we had decided to paint the woodwork that color, which was Mum's favorite. When it was all done there had been a little paint left over, so my dad slapped it on the wall in my room. I remember I liked it so much it was almost a year before he papered over it.

"So that's why you wanted this room, eh?"

I nodded. It was nice to be back in my old place again,

with its funny slanting ceiling, old shuttered window, and spectacular view over the fields.

It was when I moved over to take in that view again that I saw the car heading our way.

"Someone's coming."

Casey shot up immediately and almost knocked me flying in his haste to get to the window, but when the car got closer and he saw it clearly, he moved back to the bed and sat with his feet up.

"Just some local yokel." He sighed and I believed he was right. It wasn't a flashy car like the sleek black Jag that had parked outside Gran's house, or the sporty red one that belonged to the man at the hotel. Just an ordinary-looking family sedan. Old and rusting.

I watched from the window as it pulled into the yard and a middle-aged guy in shabby coveralls got out.

Casey stayed where he was when I went down to see what the guy wanted. He was always wary of people he didn't know and was never comfortable with strangers. My problem is that I'm not wary enough. When the man told me his car had overheated, I took it in like a wet sponge and let him waltz into the living room like he was one of the family. I didn't even look at the car—which if it were overheating as badly as he said, would have been steaming, I guess. He just looked so ordinary. I sound like some old dear who's just been conned out of her life savings: *He looked so honest, officer. I'd never have guessed he was a crook.*

I don't know what I was expecting. Perhaps MEMBER OF A MURDEROUS UNDERGROUND GANGSTER MOVEMENT tattooed across his forehead might have helped, but then again maybe even that wouldn't have been enough—I was so gullible then, I can hardly believe it now. One thing's for sure, though—I'll never be that naive again.

Even when he reached into his inside pocket and pulled out the gun, it took a few seconds for it to sink in. At first I thought it was some kind of cheap practical joke.

Casey came down when I called him. I didn't want to, but when you've got a loaded revolver pressed against your head it's hard to think straight and you usually do what you're told or end up with your brains dripping down the wall behind you. As we moved out into the yard I remember thinking that this must have been how Casey felt the day I pulled the prop gun on him. Now that I knew what it was like, I realized why he had looked so nervous.

We did as the guy said when he told us to march towards the car. I didn't want to because lately it seemed like every time we got into a car, or on a train, we were just traveling deeper and deeper into an impossible situation, and the further we traveled, the harder it was becoming to find our way back.

I guess I must have been walking really slow because I felt a sharp pain in my back, and suddenly found myself moving fast towards the car. I'm not really sure what happened next. I was still in a bit of a daze; everything was happening so quickly lately, it had been like one of those endless nightmares where just when you think you're going to wake, something worse happens and you begin to believe it's never going to end.

I must have hit the car with some force, because the pain that ran through my chest as my ribs collided with the side-view mirror was unbelievable. The only way I can describe it is to say, try and imagine toothache ten times as bad, spread across your chest. When I looked up my eyes were blurry and I could barely make out the two shapes of Casey and the other guy. When I was pushed forward Casey must have made a move for the gun because it looked like they were struggling. One was pushing the other against the car and my vision was so hazy I couldn't tell who was who. I couldn't stand, either, but somehow managed to scramble away just as they shuffled towards me—if I hadn't, they would have crashed full on top of me, and at that time I was in no state to have three hundred pounds drop full on my chest.

I made it to the corner of the yard and tried to find something that I might be able to tackle the man with and knock him out. I still couldn't see too well, a brilliant ball of white light appeared everywhere I looked, but it was getting smaller and less intense and I began to make things out around the edge of it. There was something which looked like a metal bar to my left, but when I reached for it, it turned out to be the kitchen drainpipe and it was secured tightly to the wall. I'd started to look for something else when I heard the sound of something dropping to the ground. Out of the corner of my eye, where my sight was best, I caught sight of it. It was the gun, only a few feet away. The barrel of it was pointing straight at me. If it had gone off when it hit the ground it would probably have killed me, and I'd have been just another statistic on a Collective computer disk.

Casey was still struggling. My vision was improving and I could now make out who was who. The guy in the coveralls was leaning against the car and was trying to hold Casey in some kind of wrestler's neck lock.

"Shoot!" Casey shrieked at me.

The gun felt strange in my hands. It was a lot heavier than I had expected. My blank-firing replica is light in comparison. Casey shouted again; this time his voice sounded higher—more choked. I had heard him the first time but it hadn't really sunk in.

"Shoot him, damn it!"

This time it hit home. He was telling me to aim that very real gun at some guy I knew nothing about and casually squeeze the trigger. He wasn't simply asking. It was a desperate plea from someone who was slowly being choked to death.

I could easily have shot the man. My eyesight was almost back to normal and incredibly, my hands held the gun as steady as they ever could have; but before I had time to squeeze the trigger, the "If only"s began to come.

If only I could hit the guy and be sure I wouldn't kill him.

If only he would stop when he saw the gun.

If only I had the guts!

If only I hadn't skipped school and gone to the library that day, I wouldn't be faced with the decision of having to take the life of a complete stranger, to save the life of the best friend I ever had.

I fired the gun, high in the air where I knew it would do no harm. The deafening noise it made made me feel like crying. I felt so helpless.

I fired again and tears began to run down my face.

Again, and more tears came. Not sad tears but hot, angry

tears that made my fury worse. And still I couldn't shoot the bastard.

I threw the gun to the ground with a gutteral, anguished cry, and fighting the pain in my chest, got to my feet. The guy was still struggling with Casey and his back was turned as I shuffled over and threw the hardest punch I ever could have. A once-in-a-lifetime blow powered by so much confusion and anger and hatred it was enough to bring the man down, but before he fell—in more of a reflex action than anything else, his body spiraled around towards me and his clenched hand caught my temple.

I vaguely remember tumbling backwards, then moments later found myself leaning against the wall of the house trying to figure out where I was and why my head felt so strange. It wasn't so much pain, as shock; as if my head had just taken fifty thousand volts and still throbbed from the aftereffects. My hand felt strange, too, but that was just because it had come to rest in the kitchen drain which was blocked with dead leaves and stagnant water.

Casey wasted no time in going for the gun. I noticed him the same instant I saw the guy lying by the car. He was on his side, hunched over holding his gut and making a strange croaking sound.

When Casey picked up the gun he gave me a puzzled look, like he wanted to know why I hadn't fired it. I think if I had been in his position he would have done so with little hesitation.

"Dirty stinking bastards."

Back in the house, Casey began pacing around the living room with the fast, anxious steps of a person trying to make a difficult decision quickly. He was mumbling to himself so fast and wild I couldn't understand most of it. The only words I really caught were the swearing curses he spat out every two seconds or so. Words that wouldn't have been out of place in a barroom brawl.

I sat on the arm of the chair trying to regulate my breathing. My ribs still felt tender and sore, and every time I inhaled too deeply it sent a sharp pain stabbing into my chest.

Casey continued cursing.

We had tied the guy into his car with some wire and tape we'd found in my dad's old workshop and we were now trying to work out what to do next. He was coming round by that time, but he wasn't screaming and struggling like I thought he might. He just lay slumped back in the seat. Totally silent, looking roughly the way I felt: kind of dazed and sick. I wasn't angry any more. It had all burned away and now all I felt was exhausted. Casey's anger remained though and it smoldered like a burning fuse. I couldn't blame him. He had been through so much lately, he had a right to feel the way he did; this time he had come uncomfortably close to being choked to death, and yet now he didn't have the hurt look he'd had at the hotel. He just looked tired.

Tired, sick and above all, angry.

"It's no use," he was saying—more to himself than me. "We can't keep running. We've got to go back . . . go back and fight them."

I sat up. "Fight them!"

He continued to pace.

"It's the only way, Jim. You know we can't talk to them, and hiding's useless."

"So what do you suggest?" I asked. There was a lot of truth in what he had just said, but I couldn't take his solution seriously. "Pick them off one by one? We're already one down, so that only leaves . . . what, fifty or so to go?"

"I don't know," he snapped—almost yelled—irritably.

His pacing became faster and he continued in silence for what seemed like ages. I wished he would stop. It was beginning to get to me. He didn't, but eventually he changed direction and as he moved through the doorway into the hall I heard him say, "I can't think in here," and a moment later the front door opened—and closed and then he was gone.

I didn't try to stop him. I figured a walk outdoors would cool him off. It wouldn't have been obvious to everyone but I could tell he was still fuming inside and if he continued the way he was going, he might do something we would both regret.

So I was left with the gun and took first watch over the guy in the car. I watched from the living room window—though it wasn't really necessary; Casey had fastened so much wire and tape around him, he now looked more like something out of an Egyptian pyramid than a middle-aged man in coveralls.

Casey was gone longer than I'd expected. About three hours, according to my watch, and at the time it seemed a whole lot longer. At first I did all sorts of pointless things in an attempt to make the time pass quicker; crazy things that normally I'd never dream of doing. I tried to tune the piano using an adjustable wrench to work the strings tighter, but I abandoned that when it began to sound so bad it was painful to listen to and it was only a few minutes after I gave up the piano as a lost cause that I suddenly had an insane urge to paint the ceiling—which was now a dirty yellow instead of a brilliant white I remembered it being. I suppose I would have done it, too, if I'd found some paint. Instead I had to settle for cleaning the stove, and when that was done and I couldn't think of anything else, I moved back into the living room and sank into Casey's chair and replayed over and over everything that had happened. I was glad I hadn't had to shoot that guy. I tried to imagine how I'd be feeling now if I had: full of remorse? Numb? Suicidal? Homicidal? I didn't know.

I just couldn't imagine killing anyone, and at that time I figured that if I couldn't shoot someone to save Casey's life, I'd never be able to do it.

Casey returned looking a whole lot calmer—almost serene. He settled in his chair and, taking in the familiar view, said casually that he had figured everything out, that it was all settled and that we should be ready to leave in two days' time. He didn't explain what his plan was, or why he chose two days to carry it out, except to say half-heartedly that that would be about the time when the groceries would run out. Every time I tried to ask about it he would tell me to relax, that he knew what he was doing, and if I pressed any further he'd tell me that I didn't know the people we were dealing with and that I should leave it to someone who did. In the end I gave up asking and so for the next couple of days I had to play watchdog and babysitter to the guy in the car. I let him out when he needed the bathroom and I wasn't really worried about untying the wires because Casey covered me with the gun, and if someone was holding a gun on *me* with a look as wild and angry as the glare Casey had when he saw that guy, I wouldn't have dreamed of trying anything. When he got back in the car I rearranged the wire so that I could free his left hand just enough for him to be able to spoon down the food I took out each time Casey and I ate. I didn't like doing it, but we couldn't let him go back and even though I hated him and everything he stood for, I couldn't just sit and watch him starve. To do that would bring me down to his level, and right then I honestly believed I'd rather have died than have that happen.

When the day to leave finally arrived, I put what food there was left in the car with him and just prayed he wouldn't get free before Casey had sorted everything out with his associates in the Collective. The journey back seemed much quicker. It usually does. We drove in silence a lot of the way because I knew it was pointless asking Casey what he had in mind, and yet it was bothering me so much I couldn't think about anything else. If he were going to tell me, he would. If he had decided not to, no amount of questioning would change his mind. I was certain of that, but as we got closer he started to fidget; he began to drum his fingers on the dashboard and look nervously around as if we were being followed. Something made me think he was itching to say something. That now he wanted to tell me his epic scheme. We were about five miles from town when he began.

We had been driving in silence for about five minutes and I can't remember how we got onto it, but the last subject we had talked about was school and for some reason

Casey kept going on about history in particular. He kept coming out with gems like: "History's a lot better than geography" and "You can learn a lot from what happened in the past."

I thought he had dropped the subject with the Battle of Hastings, then right out of the blue he said, "Ever heard of the Gunpowder Plot?"

"Yeah." I nodded. Apart from William the Conqueror and Henry VIII, Guy Fawkes is one of the only historical characters I know a bit about. I missed quite a few history lessons.

"That's the plan."

When it sank in, I said, "Oh, I see," in mock surprise and then added with a sarcastic grin, "You're planning to blow up the Houses of Parliament!"

I'm not usually as sarcastic as that, but there had been a lot of tension in the car and it had been an opportunity for a little light relief I couldn't resist.

Casey looked at me but didn't return my grin.

"So to speak," he said and I sat looking at him, waiting for some kind of punch line.

It never came.

Turning his head, he fixed his gaze on the white center line and it seemed to hold him in a sort of hypnotic trance. His eyes never left it, and yet he began to speak as if he were seeing something beyond—as if he were watching the things he was telling me being acted out on some imaginary stage that only he could see.

"The first Tuesday of every month, the Collective meets in their headquarters downtown. It's the one big meeting where they discuss all the main issues, and the things they can't talk about over the telephone. We're probably top of the bill this month. Everyone goes. The people who know it call it the monthly gestapo meeting.

"Next to the conference room where it's always held, there's a storeroom. All we have to do is plant a batch of explosives in there, and any time between seven and ten, when the meeting is in session, crawl through the window and light the fuse."

I suddenly felt cold and shivered violently. "Explosives?" I managed to say, but wasn't sure he had heard. It came out weaker than I had intended.

He heard. "Dynamite. From the quarry. There's enough in the back of this car to flatten a whole block." He spoke the words like he was reading them off a cue card. Coolly. Impersonally. And he meant them.

He was serious! I had actually been stupid enough to believe that he had figured out some reasonable solution to a totally unreasonable situation—blind enough not to question it, and when he came out with this crazy, crackpot scheme I just knew he was serious. That that was it. No instant solution. No magic wand that would put everything right. He was honestly planning to do everything he had said.

"It isn't going to work," I said and was amazed at how calm my voice sounded. Not the high, ear-piercing shriek of *Are you crazy?* I first felt. Just quiet, collected reasoning.

"Look, Jim." He tore his eyes from the road as he told me for about the hundredth time that I still didn't know what we were dealing with. The words grated on me so much I shuddered.

"We're not playing by the rules any more," he went on.

"It's a fight to the death and it's either them or us."

Despite the urge to push the brake pedal through the floor, I kept on going forward.

Casey turned back to the road and we traveled the next few miles in a kind of stunned silence. I shuddered again and tried hard to force my mind away from all the dreadful thoughts that had begun running through my head, but it seemed the harder I tried to blot them out, the stronger they became. In spite of everything I found myself thinking about the dynamite. I began to wonder how much was in the back of the car and just how Casey had managed to smuggle it out of the quarry. I didn't know much about the place but I figured they would keep their explosives locked safely away. You couldn't just walk in and help yourself. Everyone knows that.

"The dynamite . . . how . . ." I eventually heard myself say after another mile or so of silent driving, and in one smooth action Casey pulled from his pocket the leather wallet of picklocks and threw them on the dash. I quickly glanced from them to him and back to the road and was thinking of asking more when he cut in with a dismissive wave of his hand.

"Piece'a cake," he began and continued with what sounded like pride in his voice. "Sunday, you see. Hardly anyone about. The only really tricky part was getting into the main compound. I had to distract the guard for that."

I had asked how before I even knew I'd said it. I wasn't too sure I wanted to know. I remembered the quarry from the times we hiked past on our way to Elmwood Brook, one of Mum's favorite spots. At the top of the quarry, where the land leveled out, was a flat area about the size of a football field, where, according to my dad, they stored all the flatbeds and bulldozers when they weren't in use. The area was enclosed by a tall wooden fence, about six feet high, and above that ran another foot of twisted barbed wire.

That compound always reminded me of a prisoner-of-war camp—the sort of place you would expect people to break out of, not in to.

"Set fire to the portable toilet," Casey casually answered my question and my stomach suddenly heaved like we'd hit a dip in the road. I don't know if it was real or imagined. It was hard to tell; things were getting so confused and my head had started to spin.

I cranked open the window in an attempt to ease the pounding and looked at a cluster of trees in the distance.

I wished I were among them. They made me think of the day I fell from the old twisted cedar at the back of the house at Malton—I almost broke my leg that day and it struck me as strange that I was looking back on such a painful, frightening experience as that with a feeling something similar to longing.

"The rest was easy . . ." Casey's voice shattered my thoughts again as he went on about the quarry. Of how he had worked the two locks to the explosives store so easily it was criminal. And how everyone seemed too caught up in the fire to notice a kid with a sackful of dynamite, roughly equivalent to the blast force of a Pershing missile, scurrying from the grounds.

Dark clouds began to form on the horizon as we moved closer to town.

The clock tower said it was 12:15 P.M. when we pulled

into the station parking lot. We hadn't spoken much; Casey had been thinking of how he was going to smuggle the dynamite into the storeroom, and I had been racking my brains trying to come up with some way—any way—that would solve the whole mess without him having to do it.

After almost fifteen minutes, the only thing I could think of that wasn't as harebrained an idea as his, was to turn ourselves in and tell the cops everything that had happened. At least they'd give us protection. I'd been thinking about it a lot lately. Stabbing that guy at the hotel had been self-defense. We *had* to give ourselves up before it turned to murder.

Casey laughed at the suggestion as he stared out of the window, watching people as they scurried around laden with baggage, like thousands of giant worker ants, all busy with their own important cause.

"Self-defense still counts as manslaughter," he began softly—almost inaudibly. "That means prison . . . My dad . . ." he hesitated. Swallowed and his face paled.

I stared at him silently. All during the long days we spent at the house he rarely mentioned his parents. Was always quick to avoid the subject.

"My dad died in prison . . . being locked away like that, it killed him. I swear to God, Jim, I'd rather die than have it happen to me. It would kill me too."

His head turned towards me and I stared into those big brown eyes. The eyes of a frightened child.

"But fighting isn't the answer."

"Not for you, but it's the only choice I have. I'm not going to let them lock me away."

"You're not old enough for that, Case. Not prison . . . I don't know, aren't there special places . . ."

I rambled on. Saying anything. Saying nothing. I didn't know what I was talking about anymore. I wished I knew what was going on. Driving back I had thought that the nightmare was ending, that I was about to wake up with everything solved. Now it seemed blacker than ever, and worst of all, deep down, I was beginning to believe that Casey just might be right. Maybe there was no choice.

I parked the car in a quiet area at the back of the station, and we both got out without a word. I wanted to say more—even started to, but the words caught in my throat and were quickly swallowed.

As I walked away, Casey was lifting from the trunk of the car a gray canvas sack—about the size of a pillowcase—with the words DEACHER'S QUARRY stenciled on the side in a sickening creamy yellow color.

I walked in a kind of daze as people on their way to the station pushed and jostled past me, and I had the awful feeling that every one of them was staring at me. Perhaps at a patch of dried blood on my shirt that I'd been too preoccupied to notice. Or maybe it was just my face: a picture seen on the front page of every newspaper in the country. I felt like a three-year-old lost among the crowds of a sold-out football play-off.

The crowds thinned out as I moved away from the station and I realized no one had been looking at me. No one had pulled at my arm and screamed for someone to call the cops as I thought they might. And I felt a whole lot better when I noticed the front page of the local newspaper covered a story about a leak of radioactive waste from the nearby nuclear plant and not of a hunt for two murderous arsonists.

My pace slowed the farther I walked and I had to force

myself to keep going. Something inside kept telling me to stop, that I should turn back and try to talk to Casey one last time. I wanted to—almost did, but deep down I realized that it would do more harm than good. I knew that the more I'd say no, the more Casey would say yes. That's the way Casey was; the harder you tried to convince him that something was wrong, the more he'd believe that it was right. The only thing you could do was to drop the subject and just hope he'd see reason in his own time.

This time though I didn't just hope. I prayed.

I got to thinking as I made my way through the quiet side streets how I felt before all this began: when I was staying with Gran everything had become so boring and routine, I kept wishing for something to change, for something different to happen. Now that it had—I laughed out loud at the understatement, and three women who were talking on the street corner turned and stared—now that it *had* changed I just wanted everything to be back to normal.

So now I knew that old saying was true: about not knowing what you have until you lose it. Two weeks ago I lost the comfortable, ordered life I had become so used to, I'd begun to hate it. And now I wanted it back more than anything else I could think of.

And here I was at last.

Gran was knitting a shapeless, oversized pullover in a repulsive Day-Glo green-colored wool while the dog scraped its flea-ridden coat backwards and forwards across the living room doorjamb until the skin beneath its coat shone.

The note Gran had written me two weeks earlier, saying she was out shopping and that dinner was in the oven, was still wedged in the frame of the big oval mirror which hung from the wall.

At least nothing had changed here. After cooking me an awful lunch which I didn't recognize and couldn't be bothered to ask about, Gran got on at me about going off without a word. Then after not much more than five minutes' reprieve—while she checked the dog for ticks—she started nagging again about leaving the place in such a state, and for not bringing a new teakettle like I said I would. I'd forgotten about that, but I guess that's hardly surprising under the circumstances. I didn't tell Gran why I'd been so wrapped up in things that I forgot. Just said I was sorry and she shook her head the way she does when the dog completely ignores her commands and starts acting goofy in public.

She never mentioned the cops though, so I figured they hadn't traced the dead guy to me yet. If they had I'd never have heard the last of it; Gran couldn't bear scandal. That's why I wanted to tell her. To have her hear it the way it really happened and not have to read some version distorted and stretched in order to sell as many copies of the local rag as possible. But I didn't. Couldn't.

Instead I sank into the chair in front of the living room fire, closed my eyes and tried hard to blot everything out. Just for ten minutes I wanted to relax. To sit back like normal people and not have to worry about the police or the Collective. Or Casey.

I honestly didn't care what happened next. The cops could lock me away. The Collective could work me over. Right then it didn't matter; I would have sold my soul for ten minutes' trouble-free thought.

I fell asleep in the flickering glow of the fire, listening to the comforting sound of Gran's knitting needles clicking together.

The next thing I heard were four loud cracks; sharp as gunfire.

Before I woke I had been dreaming: I was running along some dark, endless tunnel and someone was following me. I didn't know who or why, but I knew they were getting closer and the harder I tried to run, the slower I moved. It was like trying to run in waist-high water.

I woke to the sound of the gunfire and sat up with a jolt, as if I'd just received an electric shock.

How much of it was a dream, I wondered, as I tried to stifle a yawn.

Then the gunshots came again.

No. Not gunshots. I looked out of the window, the direction from which the sound had come and saw someone outlined against the last of the day's sunlight. Whoever it was, was rapping on the glass with something metal. A coin.

The window slid open before I could reach it, and the person with the coin crawled in.

Casey.

At least that part of the dream was real.

"You should get that catch fixed," he said as he eased the window down. "There's a lot of crooks around here."

I didn't doubt that. Not anymore.

Sauntering into the room, he cut a large piece of fruitcake from a tray on the table, then sank into the chair I'd just gotten up from and asked how I was doing.

"Fine," I lied and hoped I didn't look and sound as bad

as I felt. Casey looked the way I wished I felt. New shirt. Clean hair. Bright-eyed and alert.

I dropped onto the sofa feeling like death warmed over and looked at the TV. It was still on. Gran must have left it on when she went out, but whatever she had been watching must have finished. Now there was just a boring current-affairs show on, where some funny-looking fellow from one of those screwed-up banana republics was ranting on about the evil dictatorship there. All heart-wrenching stuff I suppose, but nothing I hadn't heard a hundred times before, and right then I figured I had enough problems of my own to think about without *that* burden too. I had just gotten up to switch it off when something the guy said caught my attention. Casey's too because he looked at me and repeated it, word for word.

"A system that is intrinsically evil cannot be reasoned with or reformed. It has to be destroyed."

"Is the Collective intrinsically evil?" I asked as I hit the off button.

"They push heroin to ten-year-old kids. I'd say that comes close enough. What would you say?"

"Two wrongs don't make a right," I replied a little too quickly—almost without thinking, and I suddenly realized I sounded like a teacher I knew a year or so back.

His name was McGregor and officially his subject was English literature. Unofficially though, it was social Responsibility: small *s*—capital *R,* as he'd chalked it on the board almost every lesson. We'd always start the class routinely enough, by talking about something we had read or discussed the week before, then within less than ten minutes he'd have swept that completely aside and we'd be getting a lecture on something totally unrelated: *Romeo and Juliet* brought a forty-minute sermon on the breakdown of family communications. *Treasure Island*—the evils of drink.

A little mixed-up, I suppose, but as far as I can remember, McGregor's was the only class I ever really enjoyed—even if I didn't pass the final exam at the end of it. No one ever did. At the close of term nobody in the class was the least bit wiser about the great classics of the English language, but we all knew why it was wrong to spit in public and how the decline of the inner cities had led to the soaring crime rate we were now faced with.

"But would it make another wrong?"

Casey's voice brought me back to the conversation I guess I'd been trying to avoid.

I hesitated.

Of course it was wrong. Wasn't it?

Then why hesitate?

Because, I told myself slowly, with deliberate calm, that it wasn't a question that could be answered lightly. If at all.

But yes . . . If there are other ways to deal with it, then . . .

"Yes, Casey, it's wrong." I rushed the words out quickly, as soon as they entered my head so I'd have no time to change them.

Then I laughed.

I couldn't believe I was having this conversation. I was fifteen years old. Last year I talked about cars and music and girls—not about whether it was morally OK to destroy a system that was intrinsically evil.

Fourteen was such a nice age. Easy. Uncomplicated.

I guess I must have reached that "difficult age" adults are always talking about.

"This is totally crazy," I almost shrieked as I moved from the window to the door opposite, then back to the window again. I just couldn't sit still. There were twinges of pain from where I'd hit the car, but they were the least of my problems and I pushed them to the back of my mind.

"There has to be some other way, Casey. The police? The guy you stabbed at the hotel was going to kill you. You had to do it. There was no other choice. They'll understand . . . You've got the wound to prove it . . ."

Words began rushing out of my mouth so fast I hardly knew I was saying them. "They'll take it all into account. Hell, mass murderers get away with little more than suspended sentences these days. Please, Case. Think about it. It's the only sane thing to do."

I crashed exhausted onto the sofa and tried to regulate my breathing again. I could feel the pain in my chest getting worse.

Casey didn't say anything. Just stared at his reflection in the brass coal scuttle by the fire and sighed.

I didn't say anything because when you're about to make the biggest decision of your entire life, you need peace to think. Time to decide.

For almost five minutes he sat by the fire, studying the face reflected in the lacquered brass of the scuttle. Silently. Intensely. And then finally he slowly raised his head, turned robot-like, and directed those dark, sad-looking eyes at me.

"But what if . . ." *Click.*

The front-door lock turned. The door opened, and slammed shut, in the same instant Casey's mouth shut tight.

"Jim?"

Damn it. Gran was back.

I thumped the arm of the sofa so hard I heard something crack.

If only she'd come back five minutes later.

If only . . .

"If only" has to be the most pointless phrase in the English language. It should be abolished—never have been invented. It's just a waste of breath because it doesn't change a damn thing.

By the time Gran had hung her coat in the hall and made her way into the living room, the window was open and Casey was gone. Gran closed the window and said it was raining.

I hadn't noticed. I was thinking.

It was like Piccadilly Circus on a busy night. People kept milling in and out nonstop. Complaining about petty little things like stolen bikes and the noise neighbors were making, and they were getting quickly taken care of. I had been in the police station for more than fifteen minutes and no one had spoken a word to me since I was told to take a seat, when I got there. (I reckoned it was some kind of police psychology, and concentrated all my energy on acting calm and relaxed: it was probably the hardest part I've ever had to play.)

When I eventually did get to see someone—a weird-looking fat guy with thick-rimmed glasses and a heavy black moustache (which made him look more like Groucho Marx than a cop)—all he wanted to know was why I hadn't been at school for so long. Keeping Casey's name out of it, I told him everything that had happened and I might as well have saved my breath. He didn't believe a word of it.

First of all he took off his glasses, and as he wiped them he told me that they had no information of any organization calling itself the Collective. Criminal or otherwise, to him it simply did not exist.

"They don't advertise in the national press," I said.

I guess it would make his job so much easier if gangsters still went around in pin-stripe suits and two-tone spats, maybe even the odd submachine gun stashed inside an innocent-looking violin case might help too.

After replacing his glasses he looked me straight in the eye for the first time, and as he leaned back in his chair announced smugly that the police had no record of anyone found injured or dead at the hotel up in Greenvale.

"They got rid of the body." I shrugged matter-of-factly as I spoke my thoughts. And he gave me the same sort of impatient grin that nurses use on senile geriatrics who are becoming too difficult to handle.

Handing me a piece of photocopied legal-sized paper taken from a red folder on his desk, he told me to read it. It was a note the school's truant officer had passed on to him, with remarks from my principal who had told her:

1. I didn't concentrate hard enough.
2. I spent too much time daydreaming.
3. It had become so bad lately that I sometimes lacked a firm grip on reality.

That wasn't true of course. Just because a person chooses

not to worry himself into an early grave over the tiniest, most insignificant things—like getting projects in on time, or remembering which color socks are and are not permitted on the school premises—it doesn't mean they lack a firm hold on reality, does it?

But it didn't really matter anyway. The guy didn't believe what I'd told him and that was that. And to be honest I can't say I blame him. I mean, if *I* still find it hard to believe, how can I expect others to?

Shortly after that the guy let me go. He had a run-over dog to deal with.

I suppose I should have been relieved to walk out of the police station a free person. I wasn't. In fact, I felt worse than ever. As if now I were carrying around a heavy weight that I just couldn't shrug off.

Thinking about it, I guess its name was Casey.

The time was 6:47 P.M.

6:47 P.M. on the first Tuesday of the month.

Right up until 6:45 I believed the cops would help.

I'd never wanted to get them involved but I'd kept it in the back of my mind as a sort of last resort—a trump card I could throw down if things got really out of hand.

It was only when I stepped from the warm station into the chill of the night that it finally dawned on me. I'd gone in there, played my trump and it hadn't worked.

It hadn't worked.

It was cold on the street. It was raining and I was thirty minutes from the Collective's headquarters. Maybe twenty if I ran and took the shortcuts through the side streets and across the iron foundry.

I ran. Far too fast for the distance I had to go, because

by the time I'd reached the alley between the milk-bottling plants of the town's dairy—which was about the halfway point—I was wiped. My breathing had become loud and rasping, and I was working my arms around like an Olympic sprinter, but I wasn't going any faster than walking pace. It was as though I were living out the dream I'd had only hours earlier—instead of a long, dark tunnel, I was running along a long, dark alley—but the feeling was the same: pushing hard and yet getting nowhere.

I wanted to stop. Just for a minute or so. To curl up right there in the gutter listening to the quiet clink of the bottles parading inside the factory, with the sickly sweet smell of sour milk in the air. Yet something kept me going. Hidden stores of emergency adrenalin perhaps?

Sheer terror more likely: Casey said a lot of things he didn't mean. That's just the way he was—talking about things he wasn't really serious about got him through the day. He also said things he really meant and sometimes it was kind of difficult to know which was which. But this time I knew that what he had said earlier was the truth, the God's honest truth. He meant what he had said, and unless I stopped him, he'd do it.

He wasn't insane. He had just been pushed too far.

Casey rarely spoke of his association with the Collective—except for the time when we were traveling to Greenvale by train, when I thought I had the right to know how I'd got myself into this mess—so I didn't know how rough it had been for him. Bad I was sure. How bad I wasn't, but I figured you would have to push someone right to the limit before they resorted to the kind of action Casey had planned.

Just before I reached the iron foundry I developed a stitch in my side. Our old PE instructor used to call them the runner's nightmare and now I could see why. Usually I stop running before one develops, but this time I continued.

Five more minutes, that's all it would take. Five minutes of excruciating pain *had* to be better than a lifetime of regret. And yet another "If only" to dwell over at TV sign-off time.

I cleared the wall of the foundry and splashed to the other side, almost falling into one of the deep pools of rainwater that covered the yard's cratered surface.

Crossing the yard was like doing a martial-arts *kata*. One false move and I could have broken an ankle, or at the least ended head-to-toe in one of the deep, oily black pools.

The gate at the other side of the yard was locked.

I could have screamed my guts out. I had taken the short cut through the foundry at least a dozen times before then, and the gate had always been open. Tonight it had on it one of the biggest padlocks I have ever seen in my entire life.

Because the yard of the foundry sloped, the wall was higher at this side. About eight feet and almost impossible to climb because the surface was so smooth—no crevices where you could get a good grip and push yourself up.

To double back would take another five minutes. I had to climb the gate. As I touched its icy surface, I felt the back of my neck crawl and vividly recalled stories I had been told at school ever since I started.

The yard itself had a bad enough reputation. That had never bothered me before. But the gate . . .

The gate was about four feet wide and just a little shorter than the wall itself. The solid vertical bars were rusty and jagged, and every one was tapered to a decorative point, twenty-six in all, and from where I was standing they looked as sharp as spearheads and just as lethal.

. . . The gate—that was totally taboo. I've heard stories of impaling and maiming that would put you off corned-beef hash for life.

Then I remembered Casey and forced all thoughts of those stories aside and began to climb.

The hinges of the gate were worn and had loosened over the years, and the gate rocked precariously as I grasped it with both hands and tried to find a toehold.

Even though I knew it was cold, the coarse, rusty surface of the iron felt burning hot under my hands.

My foot found a notch in the metal. Lost it. Found it again and lost it a second time. If only I'd worn my Nike trainers, they would have gripped it.

I ignored the burning sensation and pulled myself higher with my hands and my right foot found a different notch. A deeper one. I wedged the heel of my shoe in, pushed up with my knee, and was able to slacken my grip on the metal. My hands would be blistered tomorrow, I knew that. But tomorrow, I told myself, was years away. Tonight was forever.

My left foot rose past the right and as it pushed onto the horizontal crossbar at the middle, the gate swung violently back, almost throwing me off balance. My hands tightened around the metal again as my feet began scrambling for a hold.

Nothing.

The bars higher up were smoother than at the bottom, because the crates that crashed into the gate stacked up to three feet at their highest. Above that no chips had been hacked into the metal. There was no choice. My feet were slipping. My hands were raw. I knew I had to throw myself over now, or drop defeated into the yard below.

Before I had time to consider the consequences of dropping eight feet onto solid concrete, I swung myself over and prayed I would clear the spikes.

My left calf caught one and for that instant it was as if time stood still. I envisioned the spike slicing smoothly through to the bone and it made me remember something I thought I'd completely forgotten.

I was seven. We'd only been at the house a couple of months and I had been out collecting blackberries from the fields nearby. I kind of got carried away with the job and didn't realize how late it had got until it started getting dark. I knew Mum would be worried sick if I didn't show up by suppertime, so I decided to take a shortcut through some restricted farmland and got caught up in a thick fence of sharp barbed wire. It cut my legs to shreds and shook me up something bad. I've still got the scars.

My left foot hit the ground first. It twisted momentarily before my knees gave way and the momentum carried me forward into the flooded road.

I was soaked to the skin, but I'd made it.

Made it—unscathed, I thought, apart from a mild ache in my left ankle and that was minor compared to the screaming pain the stitch still caused.

Back at school they told us the only cure for a stitch was to run.

I ran. Only vaguely aware of the warm sensation where my calf had brushed against the spike. Not knowing (or not wanting to know) that the warmth was blood oozing from a deep, ragged cut.

My footsteps echoed around the long, narrow alley.

Fast. Beating perfect time with the ticking of my wrist-watch. Both were in perfect sync with the pounding I could feel in my chest.

By the time I'd almost reached the end of the alley, I was beginning to think that what they'd told us in school was untrue. Running didn't cure a stitch. It made it worse!

I felt like I was dying, and I guess it must have showed because when I passed one of the dark doorways where some kids were playing, I heard one of the younger ones shriek like they'd just seen a ghost or something.

I slowed down a little.

The street I turned onto next was as dark, still and creepy as anything I can ever remember seeing in the hundreds of horror films I'd seen as a morbid little kid. Water vapor, discharged from the heating systems of the big old buildings, hung low on the ground like a ghostly night mist, and the only sound was the eerie slosh of rainwater as it ebbed its way to the drain behind me.

The street itself was one of the oldest and longest in town. According to Gran it was once the smartest and richest too, but that was years ago when she was just a kid—long before the people who owned the houses had moved to the posh new mansions in the suburbs and left this once-grand but now ancient and crumbling line of broken-down buildings to be turned into apartments and offices.

The Collective's headquarters stood at the far end of the

street. Surrounded by other buildings and yet somehow standing alone—it reminded me of the spooky old house in *Psycho:* ugly, dark, and sinister. As I moved closer I felt like the character from the end of that film: sure that something awful was about to happen, but not knowing what, or how, or when it would come.

And then suddenly I knew.

Up ahead I saw it materialize out of the mist like some ghostly special effect. But this was a sight more horrific than any movie had ever produced.

It wasn't the way he staggered towards me, zombie-like. Or the way the blood seeped through his trembling white hands as they clutched at his chest. Even that I could take. It was the eyes. The way they bulged wide, like he'd just witnessed the ultimate horror. That's what shook me the most.

Casey's legs gave way as he reached me. He fell forward and almost brought us both down. I don't know how, but I somehow managed to keep my balance and carry us both to the sidewalk just as a big Esso tanker, on its way to the foundry, thundered past, spraying out water and noise from beneath its sixteen tires.

The sidewalk was icy cold and covered with water, but I only noticed it for a moment. After that I couldn't feel anything. I stared down at Casey as he looked up and began to say something.

"Didn't make it, Jim . . . Should've taken the window. Didn't even make it through the entrance before . . ."

He broke off painfully and swallowed.

"I don't know, Jim, maybe... maybe you were right..."

He breathed out the last words so quietly I had to move

my ear real close to hear. His voice was high and shaky, and he made it sound like he was apologizing for something.

I shook my head. "It doesn't matter."

Nothing much mattered anymore. I'd forgotten about my stitch—or it had gone. And my ankle didn't hurt anymore.

I guess I was using all my concentration just trying not to cry. Because crying, that means it's bad. The worst. And I didn't want Casey to know what I was thinking. Thinking, but trying hard not to.

The rain got heavier before the ambulance came, and I could have sworn there were flecks of ice in it. Casey never noticed; he'd passed out cold.

Some woman on her way to the Town Hall dinner dance made the call and the ambulance seemed to take forever. When it eventually turned up I screamed something abusive at the driver, but I can't remember what. It wasn't important. Like I said, nothing much mattered any more, and I guess that's why I didn't feel bad when I started back to the headquarters on my way home from the hospital.

It wasn't much after eight o'clock and I was about twenty minutes from the building. Even limping slowly along I knew I'd have plenty of time to reach the place, then climb through the window and finish the job Casey had started, long before the meeting was over.

The pain in my ankle—which had returned and grew while I paced the hospital waiting room—began to ease the further I walked, and as I got closer to the headquarters my steps gradually changed from a slow limping shuffle until I was moving along in fast, purposeful strides which caused the matches in my pocket to rattle in their box: I'd bought them at the hospital gift shop—though at the time I wasn't sure why. I told myself later that it was simply to pass the time. Just something to get me out of that awful place.

That horribly quiet waiting room. Silence doesn't bother me most times. Sometimes I even crave it, but when you're in a room full of people and there's not a sound, like the place is empty, that's frightening.

The big double-door entrance to the Collective's headquarters was closed. Locked, I wasn't sure—and I didn't risk trying to find out. If it were locked, there would be no point. If it were unlocked and someone was waiting inside, then I could end up in the same condition as Casey.

Critical, the doctor had called it.

I edged my way among the shadows to the back of the building—a high-walled yard where everything seemed just that much colder. A little darker and still, very still.

The window to the storeroom was one story up, just as Casey had said. Slightly to the left of a thick black drainpipe which twisted down the tall building like a fat ugly vein. I knew it was the storeroom window because it was smaller than the rest, and it was dark, next to a larger lit window (where the blinds were closed but fine slats of light still managed to break through).

And the window was closed.

Of course it was closed. I knew that now. On my way to the building my wild determination had kept me blind enough to believe that I'd have no problem getting into the place. That it would be a simple matter of walking in, lighting the fuse and walking straight back out again. But now I was faced with the stark reality of the situation. I was standing in almost total blackness, looking up to a locked window about ten feet above me, wondering how I was going to break into a place most people in their right mind would walk a mile to avoid.

The window was a lift-up sash type, similar to the porch window frames on the house at Malton. If I had Casey's wallet of picklocks, then maybe I could have worked the catch and pried it open. But I didn't have the wallet and I wasn't going back to get it. I suppose I could have made the journey with enough time to spare before the meeting was over, but I just couldn't go back to the hospital. Not then. Maybe tomorrow. It would be easier then because everything seems better in the light of day. Things are easier to handle.

I forced my mind back to the task in hand and told myself over and over that it wasn't mass murder. It was social responsibility, just like they'd taught us at school. Tuesday afternoons, fifth period. English lit. Then I remembered the picklocks Casey had shown me. Twelve in all. The one he had used on the porch windows was long and flat. Something like a spatula or thin knife blade.

I slapped my back pocket and something quietly rattled.

My rusty old penknife. I'd been carrying it around so much lately I hadn't realized it was there. I don't know why I carry it with me. It's not much use as a knife any more. It's blunt and rusty and small, and it rattles because it's not properly secured to the handle now. But that's not too surprising. I've had the thing since April 1980. My eighth birthday.

I pulled it from my pocket, opened out the blade and as I looked up to the window above me, gripped it tight between my teeth. The metallic taste it gave made me think of blood. The way your mouth feels after getting a split lip or losing a tooth.

The drainpipe was cold and wet, and climbing it was pretty uncomfortable, but not as difficult as I thought it might have been. I climbed up with a kind of wild impelling purpose, like some little kid on a dare. I guess I could have made the climb quicker if I'd needed to, but I took it slow and steady because I was careful not to make any noise that would be heard in the room next door. If anyone happened to flick open the blind and glance out to their right, they'd see me hanging there like the last pathetic turkey at a Christmas bazaar.

About eight feet from the ground the drainpipe was fastened to the wall by a sort of wraparound bracket, which was metal like the pipe and roughly an inch thick. It was just enough to support my right foot so I could push myself up until my left knee rested on the window ledge itself. That took most of my weight, and with my other foot braced on the bracket, it gave me enough stability to continue. It made me feel easier too. The same way a mountain climber must feel after reaching the last base camp before going for the summit. It made me feel like things were going really smoothly, and I guess that's why it seemed worse when I lost my grip on the knife. Without warning my stomach twisted and fell, the way it sometimes does when you travel in a fast elevator and it stops suddenly. But this seemed worse because I knew there was no elevator supporting me, just a narrow window ledge and cold damp drainpipe. For one horrible moment I thought I was going to lose my hold on the ledge, but I kept my balance and when the knife rebounded off my knee and quietly fell to rest on the splintered wood beside it, I began to breathe again.

I picked up the knife calmly. Its blade was fine enough to slip between the two halves of the wooden frame with nothing more than a gentle push, and it slid over to the center catch, smoothly and quickly. The next part took longer, but I knew from experience that it would. Out at the house when Casey was showing me how the picklocks worked, he got really tickled and eventually collapsed into a heavy fit of giggling while he watched me cursing and getting mad when I couldn't get the catch to slide quick enough. I thought he hadn't showed me right, but a few minutes later when he had controlled his laughing down to just the odd little snigger, he told me that it just wasn't something that could be done fast. It was sort of like picking lint off a wool sweater. You had to stroke the metal pick across the catch over and over, until it moved slowly and gradually. Bit by bit. If you're in a hurry, you use a brick.

That time it took about four minutes. This time it took longer. Maybe twice as long—probably because I wasn't using the correct tool, if you can call it that—but I kept with it. Stroking the knife hard across the metal with unbelievable calm. Almost worryingly cool. Until the catch slipped.

The window slid smoothly and as I dropped into the dark of the storeroom, that was when I finally broke into a heavy sweat. I just told myself it was some kind of delayed reaction to the control I'd shown outside, and as I peered around the room (which wasn't as dark as I first thought, because a thin strip of light from the corridor filtered its way under the door) I reckoned that was why my hands were shaking too.

It didn't take me long to find the dynamite. There were five bundles of six sticks pushed deep under a tall shelf unit, which stood against the wall that adjoined the conference room.

Casey had planned it well.

I pulled the matches from my pocket, took out one, and reclosed the box. That's all it would take. One tiny matchstick. The rasping sound it made as it struck against the sandpapery edge of the box sounded unreal. Sort of out of sync and far too loud in that small, silent room.

I was sure they had heard it next door.

But they hadn't.

The match slowly burned down and there was no sound of startled panic. No one running from the room to begin kicking at the door behind me.

Just horrible silence.

I picked up the thick waxy fuse in my left hand and pulled it towards me. At the same moment my right hand was moving the match slowly towards it.

Mr. McGregor once told us during one of his famous sermons in English literature, that the ability to accept responsibility for yourself and others is the great divide which separates adults from children. Sometimes the line is hazy, and some people reach it much sooner than others, but one day in our lives we all have to cross it.

I think that is probably true.

Long before I ever knew McGregor, someone else once told me that when you grow up, your soul dies. I'm not sure anymore if that's true but the thought that it could be, still scares me now, almost as much as it did then.

I've been thinking about both those things a lot lately.

The meeting finished shortly after ten o'clock and about five minutes later the light that filtered in from the hall went out as the last person left.

I remained in the dark. Sitting up against the shelves as I toyed with the matches, thinking. Or at least trying to. But like it sometimes happens when you try too hard to concentrate on something, nothing much came except for a few mixed-up images which left me more confused than ever, and after fifteen minutes the only thing I could decide on was the fact that I wasn't fit to decide anything right then.

At that moment all I wanted to do was go home and rest.

I left the headquarters by a small bolted doorway at the back of the building. It was raining heavily by then and the roads sparkled coldly with reflected light from the lamps overhead. The street was empty and still, and almost silent apart from the slosh of rain and the faint sound of people far off singing some tuneless, drunken song that I vaguely remembered. For some reason I envied them.

A car passed me on the corner at the end of the street and sprayed me with water. At least I think it was a car. Or maybe a small truck. I hadn't really noticed it much. I was thinking of other things.

Maybe I was wrong not to light the fuse. I didn't know.

It seemed like I'd been wrong about so much lately, and

I guess I just wasn't prepared to take the chance. I was wrong when I thought I didn't worry about things that mattered. Wrong when I assumed I could talk anybody out of doing anything if I tried hard enough. And I had honestly believed I had cried my last, six years ago at the only funeral I have ever attended. I'd been wrong about that too.

I suppose I should be feeling something now. Worried I guess. Maybe that will come later. I don't know how big the Collective is, or how wide it stretches, but I figure there's got to be some place they haven't reached yet, and if Case . . .

When Casey recovers, we could head for it.

Further north maybe. I don't know. I can't think about that now. At the moment all I want to do is get home and rest for a while. Just ten minutes' trouble-free thought. That's not much to ask for, is it?

But you know I still can't stop myself from thinking.

If only . . .